Willowby's World

∾

For Morgan aa Oakley

May you find joy
ad comfort i nature
throughout your lives

Best wishes

Dave Edwares

Willowby's World

❧

Deirdre Edwards

Newberry Press

Newberry Press
www.Willowbysworld.com

First published 2008

Printed in United Kingdom by CPI Antony Rowe, Eastbourne

Edited by Chris Baron
Designed by Nancy Lawrence

ISBN 978-0-9556327-1-6

A Catalogue record for this book is available
from the British Library

DEDICATION

∽

To all the children I have had
the privilege to know

CONTENTS

ꬲ

FOREWORD

And this our life exempt from public haunt,
Finds tongues in trees, books in the running brooks,
Sermons in stones, and good in everything.
The Duke; As You Like It, Act 2, scene 1

THOSE FEW LINES FROM SHAKESPEARE'S "As You Like
It" took root in my mind the day I learned them at
school. I have always found them to be true. Willowby's
World invites young readers to enter into the magical
world of nature and, like the duke, find "good in everything". Willowby, the old willow tree, provides an
opportunity for children and adults alike to return to
their original relationship with the consciousness of
nature, the greatest teacher.

FIRST INSIGHT
Life is Just a Game
~

"WHY CAN'T I? Everyone else is going."

"I told you, we can't afford it. You are not going."

"But that's what you're always saying."

"You can't go, Sonya, because we don't have any spare money."

"It's not fair! I'll be the only one not going, I'll be all left out when they talk about the trip afterwards, and it's all your fault. Daddy would let me go. I wish Daddy were here, he'd say yes, he'd let me go."

"But he's not here."

"No, and I'm stuck with you and you're always saying no. It's not fair. Nothing's fair anymore."

Sonya slammed the back door behind her and ran out of the house into the garden. Her face all red and puffy, angry tears streaming down her face, she headed straight for her special place. Beyond the gate at the bottom of the garden was a little wood and there, in a tranquil glade, beside a pretty bubbling brook stood a beautiful old willow tree. Whenever Sonya wanted to be alone, whether she was happy or sad, she always made for this tree. She loved to walk through its flowing branches and feel them brush against her. She would weave in and out of the willow's long tendrils sometimes swinging on them, and dance alone in her secret place. There she would crouch near the trunk knowing she was hidden from the whole world. Here she entered another universe, here she pondered on her life, she dreamed her dreams and she wished her wishes, here she was safe and only the willow knew her secrets.

"Life isn't fun anymore, not like it used to be," she sobbed as she grabbed hold of a supple leafy stem that seemed to be brushing her tears away from her cheek. She tugged hard and shook it with all her might. "Why is life so unfair? Why can't I have Daddy at home like everyone else?" She grabbed another beckoning branch and twisted it around her. "If Daddy were here he wouldn't say no to me all the time like Mummy. He'd let me go on the trip like everybody else. He wouldn't tell me we didn't have any money." She looked at a young sprig that was swaying in front of her. Reaching out and touching it, she inspected the veins on the young leaves. She ran her fingers along the smooth bark feeling the soft papery leaves and whispered to them, "I wish he was at home again. Why did he have to go away? Life is not the same anymore, why did he have to go away?"

In response, the tender young sprig greeted her finger-tips with a comforting warm glow that travelled up her arm, gradually permeating her whole body. Another stray tendril gently stroked her forehead. Her eyes began to feel heavy and she was overcome by a feeling of drowsiness. Flopping down onto the grass, she lay on her back, allowing the branches to gently caress her as she gazed up through the maze of green leaves to the blue sky beyond.

The willow tree looked down at her full of tenderness, swaying his branches over her, calming her hot head and tired sobs. His leaves whispered, and Sonya closed her

2

eyes and drifted into a peaceful sleep. He contemplated her tear stained face and swayed gently. Lightly twirling the tips of his leaves over her curled up form, he wove a dream into her mind.

She was four years old again, laughing her heart out and being thrown high into the air by her father. He caught her and dangled her above him, his eyes twinkling with merriment as he gazed up at his little girl.

"So you want to go to the seaside do you?"

"Yes, yes, yes, yes, yes!"

"Well have you been a good girl?"

She was now hanging precariously above his head. She stretched out to touch him but to no avail, "Yes, yes, yes."

"Are you sure?"

She felt she was about to drop and squealed with delight, "Yes, yes I promise." Now she was certain he was going to drop her. Sure enough, she was swooped down to the ground and set free. She ran from him in glee, this was her favourite bit, now he would grab her with a roar and scoop her up into a huge bear hug.

Afterwards the father held her in front him and looked at his little daughter. He smoothed her hair tenderly and thought how lucky he was to be her father. "So you want to go to the seaside?" She looked up into his eyes trustingly, knowing he would understand that it was her most desperate desire. Her eyes met his tenderness, "Well we'll see, what about this little brook here?"

"It's not the same as the sea," she looked down, determinedly avoiding his eyes.

"What about the willow tree?"

"What about the willow tree?" She looked up at her father. What had the willow tree got to do with anything?

He bent down towards her, looking deep into her

3

eyes before whispering in reply, "Don't you think he'll miss your company?"

"Miss my company? Daddy!" Little Sonya poked him and threw back her head and crowed with laughter. He was joking with her and she loved it.

"You never know," he said to her mysteriously, "think about it. Are you sure he won't miss your company?" Little Sonya looked at him. Her father was being serious.

"The willow tree?" she asked curiously.

"Yes the willow tree, Willowby the Willow Tree."

"Daddy?" she grabbed his face in both her hands to make him look at her sensibly. "Daddy!" she remonstrated with him.

"Yes," he responded looking straight into her challenging eyes, "the willow tree, Willowby the Willow Tree."

As he spoke the image of him dissolved into the willow tree.

"Daddy!"

She opened her eyes and looked directly at the trunk beside her, "Daddy!"

"He can't be with you now, but he would love to be." Sonya knew in her heart that this was true, "He loves you, and he would be with you if he could."

"I miss him," a sob of desperation lodged itself in her throat.

"I know, so does your mother."

"Not as much as me" Sonya retorted stubbornly.

"Oh yes – be patient with her," the deep friendly voice urged.

"She always says no," Sonya argued.

"She cannot say otherwise if there is no money for your trip to France."

"How did you know I wanted to go to France?" It was suddenly dawning on Sonya that this voice knew a very great deal about her.

4

The voice replied, "You told me – or at least I over-heard you."

Sonya suddenly sat up, she was certain she was no longer dreaming. Goose pimples were slowly creeping up her spine. She surveyed the trunk of the tree for some time, not daring to breathe. The willow tree, under-standing her curiosity, allowed her to peer at him. He drew himself up tall and majestic against the bright blue sky and swirled his cloak of branches around Sonya, saying nothing.

Eventually, slowly and deliberately, scrutinising the tree as she spoke, Sonya said, "I want to go to France."

"But your mother has told you that she has no money and that is true." The voice, strong and resonant, was most insistent.

Sonya sprang up and looked around, breathing loudly and feeling nervous. She was now wide awake. Where was the voice coming from? There was definitely a voice from somewhere. Somebody was talking to her and it wasn't someone inside her head.

"Why don't you want to stay here with the brook?" The voice seemed to taunt her echoing her dream.

"But that's not France," Sonya challenged disgustedly.

"What about me?"

Sonya froze, "What about you? Who are you? Where are you? What are you?" she turned slowly as she spoke grabbing hold of a waving branch for comfort, very afraid of what she might find. Was she really not dreaming?

"I'm here," replied the gentle voice, "you're looking at me, you're touching me."

Sonya looked at her hands; she noticed that both her hands were tightly clutching a slender stem of the willow tree. She stared at the leaves within her grasp, all crushed,

A deep rumbling sound emanated from the tree and
the leaves shook, it was the tree laughing, "Of course trees can
talk, but hardly anyone ever listens."

6

and she slowly took in the long supple branch as her eyes followed its length to the towering trunk, and up to the sky beyond. She gazed around her, and noticed Willowby's cloak of leaves that shrouded her from the outside world. She was overcome by the sheer presence she felt encompassing her. Her spine prickled with excitement and she released the branch from her grasp.

"You could play with me!" The deep friendly voice resonated through her.

She did not reply but looked intently at the tree.

Suddenly she gasped with delight. For a brief second the willow revealed his face to her. "I can see your face, and I never knew that trees could talk."

A deep rumbling sound emanated from the tree and the leaves shook, it was the tree laughing, "Of course trees can talk, but hardly anyone ever listens." As the quietly toned words drifted over the breeze to Sonya, she thought she detected a sad sigh sweeping through the willow's boughs.

Deeply moved Sonya responded, "Would you like me to listen to you?"

"But you want to go to France."

"Yes, but then if mummy really can't afford it..."

"Then you could stay here and keep me company."

The same excited goose pimples raced up and down Sonya's spine. Suddenly the idea of not going away seemed strangely intriguing. Certainly, none of her friends going to France had a real magical tree for a friend. She felt very special.

"I'd like you to be my friend," continued the tree, "I know all about you, I've watched you growing up, playing around me for years, and I want to be your friend."

"Oh," Sonya giggled a little shyly as she remembered

7

all the times she had spent dancing and prancing in and out of the branches, thinking she was completely alone and unobserved. She hopped from one foot to the other and then declared, "Yes Willowby, I would like to be friends, too. Willowby, is that your name?"

She shook her head in disbelief as she heard the words tumble out of her; she still could not quite believe what was actually happening.

"Yes, yes, that's right," chuckled Willowby, "I have been living beside this little brook ever since your great, great grandfather planted me here." As he spoke his deep warm voice resonated up from his roots. "It's been a long time since I had a friend to talk to, somebody who was prepared to listen to what I had to say, someone who was keen to learn."

A feeling of loneliness and sadness wafted over Sonya. She peered at the willow. For a moment she could have sworn it was weeping. "Of course your great, great grandfather was my last friend; we shared all our thoughts and ideas together in those days. There was time then; he would wander over and sit on the edge of the brook sunning himself, and we'd talk for hours. How we would talk! What a wonderful team we were. He followed all my advice; he was so good at listening and learning. Look at what he achieved in his lifetime!"

Sonya fell into a deep reverie as she heard this. She had never known this great, great grandfather of course, but there was a portrait of him in the hall in the house.

It had always been there. She had often gazed up at the kind, intelligent eyes, in that wise, old face. She pictured him now – severely dressed but with an air of humour as he looked down at her from the wall. This was the grandfather who had built the house, who had founded the school, whose name was used when the new estate was built on the other side of the village. Sonya began to daydream as her imagination transported her into that portrait…

Her great, great grandfather turned from the armchair and gazed out of the window. He could just see the outline of the willow tree.

"Ah yes," he said to himself, "the willow tree; that is where it all started." His mind cast back to a distant time when a little boy planted a single, slender stem into some soft soil beside a pretty babbling brook. The memory came to him as if it had only been the day before. Yet, before his eyes, his friend Willowby the Willow Tree, in all his mature splendour, now towered over his fellow trees in the little wood. He nodded to himself, "I have had a good life," he declared, "my children are all married and have left home, and the school is flourishing." He walked towards the mirror above the fireplace, and chuckled to himself. His piercing blue eyes sparkled back at him, "Yes," he reminded his reflection, "I am still a persistent fellow. 'Never give up on your dream' that has been my life's motto." He suddenly laughed out loud, remembering that this was one of the old willow tree's mysteries. His eyes drifted towards the window again and, shaking his head slowly, he mused, "Willowby's World. I never would have thought when I planted that young sapling all those years ago what secret wonders it would one day reveal to me." Pondering on this he straightened his shoulders, turned and fixed Sonya with a penetrating stare.

Sonya awoke from her daydream; a slow shock took root deep inside. Her head cleared, she looked up and stared steadily at the tree. Willowby the Willow met her gaze. "Are you ready to begin?"

His mirth suddenly subsided. He was now quite still, gazing tenderly down at the small figure standing bewildered before him.

"Begin, begin what?" Sonya asked, still trying to make sense of this new reality.

Willowby looked down at her with the same intensity that Sonya had encountered in the portrait of her great, great grandfather. "Let's begin at the beginning," he replied, "as with any story."

Sonya gazed up into the ancient face of the old tree searching for the truth in his words. "Was he mocking her?" Feelings of indignation began to stir within her. She couldn't bear it if he was making fun of her.

He looked down at her with utter understanding and the kindness in his eyes melted her fears, teasing the shy smile on her lips into a grin. Just then a robin hopped down in front of her. He looked straight at her and cocked his head to one side; he too seemed to expect a response from her. Suddenly that same excited tingle ran up and down her spine as the sound of the whispering leaves again rustled around her.

"Well," they bobbed and glinted excitedly at her in the sunlight, "Are you ready to play?"

"Play?" Sonya repeated, as a light breeze ruffled through her hair. Her face lit up with excitement. "Play with a tree?" she thought. "Play what?" she cried, bursting with curiosity.

"The Game," Willowby chuckled, his branches now beginning to tremble with his merry laughter.

His laugh was so infectious that Sonya, still not fully comprehending, dissolved into giggles, "G . . . G . . . Game? What game?" she remonstrated helplessly trying to tug a response from his teasing branches as they artfully darted just out of reach from her hands.

"The Game of Life," Willowby roared, his whole trunk now shaking with mirth. "All of life is a game, a

11

game, you see?" His mirth suddenly subsided. He was now quite still, gazing tenderly down at the small figure standing bewildered before him.

"What is the game, how do you play?" At that moment, of all things in the world, Sonya knew that she wanted to play that game, whatever it was. "Tell me how to play," she implored, at last succeeding in grasping a willowy branch that swung towards her.

A chill pierced her bones. The willow was towering over her, bearing down as if to peer closely into her soul. "First I need to know, are you ready?"

The question shocked Sonya but she stood her ground. Standing erect, her arms straight down by her side, she answered without any hesitation. "Of course I am, why?"

"Well, to play The Game of Life, you need to know The Golden Insights," Willowby replied seriously. He then paused before continuing gravely. "They have been guarded as a mystery."

"Why? What sort of mystery?"

"A powerful mystery. A mystery so powerful, that has been waiting for a time when it may be safe to be revealed."

"Oh." Lost for words, Sonya was barely able to speak with excitement. Then suddenly the same feeling of sadness that she had sensed earlier wafted over her, and she caught the hint of a long sigh as the tree swayed his branches before her. Willowby moaned softly in a deep flowing watery tone. "We have been passing through a long period of darkness, when few would believe, yet others were tempted to use the mysteries to seize power for their own means and enslave others."

Sonya shivered; she had not expected such an answer. Willowby looked down at Sonya as if searching for something hidden deep inside her.

She felt the intensity of his stare as she tentatively asked, "Will there ever come a time when it is safe to reveal these mysteries?"

"Soon, the time is nearly ripe," replied Willowby with an air of ancient authority.

"How do you know when that will be?" asked Sonya, intrigued.

"When people are ready," stated Willowby quite simply.

"When will you know that?" Sonya was beside herself with curiosity – she wanted to know everything.

"When people want to change, when they want things in the world to be different," Willowby replied before continuing. Closely observing Sonya's reactions to what he had been telling her, he chose the next few words carefully. "Some people are ready. They are already learning the mysteries," he paused. "Are you ready Sonya?"

"Why?" gasped Sonya, what was she going to be told?

Then an insistence urged the whisper that rustled the leaves, "Sonya, are you ready for the mysteries?"

Sonya nodded.

"You are sure?"

Sonya nodded again.

"Sure?"

"Sure," Sonya joined in.

A strong breeze blew up through the trees and around the willow, rattling his branches. "Sure!"

Sonya stretched out her hand and grasped a branch the willow was waving in her direction. "Sure," She felt a shock penetrate her outstretched hand, a shock of great strength and vitality that coursed its way up through her arm and into her heart. She stood poised before the tall willow and looked directly at him, ready for any challenge. The wind subsided.

"Alright, tell me," Sonya commanded when all was calm once more, "what are these powerful mysteries, what are 'The Golden Insights'? I want to know."

Willowby noted the change in Sonya. He smiled in acknowledgement and, after a short silence, began to explain carefully, "Think of life as a game, Sonya, The Game of Life. The Game of Life is all about using invisible laws to live your life. These laws are ancient and are known as 'The Golden Insights'. When you play The Game, you can choose either to follow The Golden Insights or not."

Willowby paused, and for a few moments Sonya thought she saw his face dissolve into the bark of the trunk. She waited; holding her breath for what seemed an age, before he continued again.

As he spoke the sun shone and the wind gently breathed through his leaves, and the babble of the brook bubbling away at his roots blended with the song of the birds in the little wood. "In this wonderful world of ours, people cannot see The Golden Insights of Life, but all of nature can."

Sonya looked around her and caught sight of the friendly robin who now appeared to be deep in conversation with two butterflies dancing above his head. From time to time he cocked his head in her direction. "Were they talking about her? What were they saying?" she desperately wanted to know. There was so much she wanted to know. She turned back towards Willowby.

Once again he was lowering his voice to the rustle of his leaves. "Remember, The Golden Insights are very powerful; they contain ancient wisdom and we trees are the guardians of that wisdom." He raised himself up, stretched out his branches and with a sudden menace shook them vigorously, demonstrating the might of his power. Leaves tumbled to the ground and came to rest at Sonya's feet. She looked down at the discarded leaves and then slowly, reverently bent down and began to pick them up one by one.

As if in response to her humble gesture, Willowby swayed deeply before her, gently sweeping the ground at her feet. His low voice resonated through every fibre of her body. "Abide by the mysteries of the old willow tree, be brave and allow the winds to sweep change into your life. For these are times of great change, this is a time of great awakening."

Mesmerised by the sensation of the words emanating from Willowby, Sonya remained crouched before the willow, barely able to move, drinking in every sound, listening intently to all that Willowby had to say. The two friends, absorbed in their conversation, lost all sense of time. The sun continued its journey across the sky; even the birds had tired of their long days singing when Sonya was brought up short by the sound of her mother's voice calling her into tea.

"Sonya," her mother was calling again.

"Oh, Willowby I must go," she cried and leapt to her feet.

"Very well," Willowby replied, "run along. We shall talk again soon, and I promise I shall share with you the mysteries of The Golden Insights."

∾

Creating Patterns
ॐ
The Magic of Human Kindness

"WHERE IS SHE?" wondered Willowby.

He was warming his old branches in the gentle yellow rays of the May sunshine, waiting for his young friend to join him. School had finished and Sonya was a little late. Suddenly he caught a glimpse of blue as she came through the back gate.

"Ah there she is," and he stretched across to try and see her better. He chuckled and thought of all the wonderful ideas he would share with her during the summer. Sonya was walking slowly in his direction, her face screwed into a frown. He smiled as he watched her dejected figure making its way towards him.

"Well?" he asked trying to catch her eye.

"Well what?" Sonya replied, hanging her head avoiding eye contact. She was going to play him at his own game today.

"How's Miss Crabface then?"

Sonya choked as her words failed her. She looked up at him; Willowby's leaves were shaking with laughter. "How did he know?" She felt foolish and cross with Willowby, "How did he know?"

She stamped her foot and remonstrated with him, "But I had done my homework and she didn't believe me. She still told me off and gave me a detention."

Sonya stood before him bewildered by his amusement. She felt hurt, Willowby was supposed to be her friend, why was he laughing at her?

Willowby plucked the last strands of her patience, "Why don't you try feeling sorry for her?" he suggested, anticipating a robust response from Sonya. He was not disappointed.

"Sorry for her? Ugh! Why?" the thought of feeling sorry for Crabface of all people; Crabface, who patrolled the school corridors looking for pupils to pounce on and punish. "Do you know, she doesn't even know what a joke is. I've never even seen her smile; I think her whole face would crack into a million pieces if she tried to smile."

Willowby chuckled at Sonya's righteous indignation.

"Now Mrs Woolley is different, she's totally different," said Sonya brightening up.

"How is she different?" Willowby asked.

"Well, when I forgot to bring my ingredients for the cake we were going to make, she just laughed and said I'd have to try and make it with leftovers, and it might taste funny."

"And did it?"

"Yes it was horrible. You ought to have seen her face when she tried it, we all fell about. Her eyes nearly popped out of her head. There was no sugar in it. I had to make a cake without sugar – can you imagine a cake without sugar?" Sonya challenged Willowby, laughing at the memory of the event at school. Then she suddenly realised that, being a tree, Willowby would never eat cake, so he probably wouldn't understand how ridiculous a cake which wasn't sweet might taste. So she quickly continued, "Anyway Mrs Woolley made a joke about my cake, and said that perhaps I should have added cheese instead and turned the dish into a savoury. But what I don't understand," and here

17

Willowby pulled himself up as high as the sky and seemed to stretch out his branches and swing them as a breeze passed lightly over him. A golden coin materialised out of nowhere and dropped into Sonya's lap.

Sonya turned her face up towards Willowby entreating him for a response, "what I don't understand is, how two people can respond so differently to the same situation. I mean I'd prepared both my homeworks; it's just that I'd left them at home. Crabface didn't believe me and got angry and gave me a detention, while Mrs Woolley just joked and tried to help me out. How is it that people react and behave so differently in the same situation, Willowby?"

A deep rumbling sound bubbled out of Willowby, he was clearly amused. "Well my friend, you have hit upon one of the great curiosities of life. In fact there is quite a simple explanation." He looked down at Sonya, her eyes were focused on him and she was listening to every word he uttered. He continued carefully, "First of all, remember those Golden Insights that I began to tell you about a few days ago?"

Sonya nodded.

"Well, it takes the experience of several lifetimes to fully understand. But I can begin to explain to you a little about how things are. Did you know," Willowby leaned down towards Sonya conspiratorially, his voice darkening with gravity, "that people reflect the nature of life, the two sides to life, the dark and the light?"

Sonya looked at him completely perplexed.

"Let me give you an example."

Willowby pulled himself up as high as the sky and seemed to stretch out his branches and swing them as a breeze passed lightly over him. A golden coin materialised out of nowhere and dropped into Sonya's lap.

Sonya gasped with astonishment at the bright coin now glinting at her.

"Take this coin," Willowby continued, "the two sides are different; on one side we have the design of the head and on the other we have the pattern of the tail – heads and tails."

Sonya picked up the coin and held it up to the sun turning it over, examining the strange patterns carved on either side.

"You see in life, like any coin, there are always two sides to everything."

Sonya frowned and shook her head; it all seemed so complicated, "I don't understand. What have the two sides of this coin to do with anything?"

Willowby cleared his throat and patiently began to explain, "These two sides represent the positive and the negative patterns in life. Everything in life is made up of these two patterns." Sonya looked around, and Willowby watched her closely as he continued, "Look out for the patterns people create around them. Are they creating positive patterns or negative patterns?"

Sonya thought about the people she knew. She thought about Miss Crabbe and Mrs Woolley, she recognised their patterns quite clearly. Then she thought about the portrait of her great, great grandfather and she asked, "How can I tell if I am creating positive or negative patterns?"

Willowby looked down at her with affection and answered gently, "When you are positive you try to be the best you can be. When you are positive you feel good about yourself. Deep inside you may feel you want to jump for joy. This is a sign that vibrant positive energy is flowing through you. While that wonderful feeling is flowing through you, you may catch yourself thinking beautiful thoughts which then create wonderful ideas that inspire you, and you take action with resounding results. When that happens, you may feel fulfilled and begin to understand that anything is possible. That is what it is like when you are dealing with positive energy and creating positive patterns."

Willowby paused. "On the other hand," he continued, choosing his words carefully, "when you are living with a negative pattern, you may find yourself trying to lead a life that goes against that wonderful energy flow. You may feel bad about yourself, you may feel nothing good is possible anymore. You may notice that life has become so stuck that very little is done, so nothing happens, and if any action is taken the results are often disappointing. That is how it can be when you are dealing with negative energy and creating negative patterns."

"I understand," nodded Sonya slowly as she weighed everything up in her mind. Then, her entire face lightening up, she leaped to her feet and declared excitedly. "Life is made up of two patterns, one is positive and the other is negative, both are different." With both hands she grabbed hold of two branches which swayed towards her and swung on them as she chanted, "I have two choices in everything, either be positive and create a positive pattern or be negative and create a negative pattern; positive or negative, negative or positive." And she leaned back, twirling the ends of Willowby's two branches around each other.

"That is correct, my dear," Willowby was delighted to see Sonya getting the point. "However," he added, "everything in life needs to be balanced, you know."

"Why?" asked Sonya, stopping in mid twirl. She gazed up at the pattern of twisted branches she had created.

Releasing them, she dropped to the ground, and watched them unravel to their own rhythm. Aware of an uncomfortable twisted knot inside her, she was both surprised and confused by this latest idea.

Willowby just swayed gently and continued, his soothing voice flowing through his branches. "You see, life is about having to balance the negative and positive. It is about learning to dance with the light and its shadow." He shivered as a passing cloud hid the sun from the world casting their tranquil little glade into shade.

"Sometimes," he continued, "it is necessary to accept the negative in life, however painful. These experiences can make us grow in strength and wisdom and so help us to appreciate the good things in life. At the same time it is also very important to recognise those thoughts that are negative and destructive, as these can destroy a person's whole life. If you are able to identify negative and destructive thought patterns, then you can decide to change them. Then the energy will flow, feelings will shift, behaviour will alter and the whole of life around you will transform."

Willowby paused, and looked down at Sonya who was sitting on the grass listening intently to all he had to say. The cloud passed on and the bright warm sun reappeared once again sharing its light and warmth. He could see that new thoughts were beginning to spin round and round inside her head, and that she was trying to make sense of them all. Willowby smiled, he knew just what to do to help her make sense of it all.

"Come on," he said, "I'll tell you a story and then you'll understand."

Sonya's face lit up, she always loved stories, and she curled up nestling her back comfortably against Willowby's wizened trunk. She felt the comforting vibration of his voice as he began....

The Magic of Human Kindness

NCE UPON A TIME, there was a young boy who lived alone with his mother and father in the middle of a wood. He was not a happy young boy, he had no friends as there was no one living nearby. He spent his days fishing in the stream, walking though the woods and talking to the trees. Occasionally he would see a stranger passing through the woods, and he would run away and hide.

Why you might ask, when he was so lonely, would he runaway and hide at the sight of another human being? Well, the answer is quite simple. He was afraid of other humans. Why was he afraid?

You see the only other humans this little boy knew were his mother and father. His mother and father didn't like each other, so they were constantly angry and bickering. They were both so cross with each other that they took it out on their son. His mother scolded him over the state of his clothes. If she asked him to cut the carrots for her, she would complain that he'd cut them up too small or too large. His father likewise, if his father sent him on an errand, he would complain that he'd taken too long. Nothing the poor boy could do was right. It was not that the parents deliberately behaved like this, you understand, it was just that they were so busy being cross with everything all of the time that they had completely forgotten how to behave in any other way.

One day, when the young June sunshine was warming the wood and playing its sunbeams over a rippling stream, a little girl was crouched at the edge of the water reaching down for the shiny smooth pebbles which lay tantalisingly on the stream bed. To her they were precious jewels which she treasured, feeling the smooth weight of them in her

hands. She had gathered a few beside her and was organis-
ing them, with great care and precision, into a particular
order which was greatly significant to her. After contemplating her ordered work she became aware that the
smooth, round, jet pebble was beckoning to her. Taking it
in her hand she gazed at it, followed its bidding, and flung
it back in the stream. The stream hit back at her, splashing
water into her eyes, making her take a step back and look
up. A magpie. Her heart missed a beat, a solitary magpie,
one for sorrow. She didn't like the feeling that began to
take grip of her. There it was again, resolutely alone. She
remembered the old law and looked quickly into the
stream and caught the sight of its reflection. Two for joy.
She ruppled the surface of the water, creating three for a
girl then four for a boy. She stopped. That was enough. She
felt the sudden cold as the sun hid behind a cloud, and she
caught sight of a fish darting to hide behind a stone. She
heard the warning croak of a frog. With utter composure,
she turned to greet the approach of the boy.

Cross and lost inside himself; she didn't fear him. She
turned from him and returned to the demands of the
order of her stones. He didn't run from her, he didn't feel
afraid of her. He noted that she was smaller than he. A
great feeling of brutish power began to course its way
through him, making him feel mighty and strong. He
observed her practising her stone ritual for a while and,
as he watched her at play, he became more and more
aware of the brutal nature of this strange new power that
was feeding his sense of personal strength.

After a few moments he strode over to her, grabbed
her by her wrist and shouted at her to leave his stream
alone. The young girl was shocked by his ferocity; his
angry grip was cutting into her wrist. "Let me go, let me

go," she cried, "you're hurting me, let go of me."

"You've no right to be playing here, it's my stream," the boy scolded her.

"What do you mean it's your stream, you stupid...." she retorted. "This stream doesn't belong to anybody. Anyone can play in it. Who do you think you are? Go away and leave me alone."

Her dark eyes blazed at him. He tried to summon his brute strength to glare back at them. He failed, and quickly turned on his heels and left. He felt angry; angry that the small girl had argued with him, angry that he had walked away, angry at the memory of her playing happily, seemingly oblivious to him.

The girl stayed. She didn't go away. She was there the next day, and the next day, and the next, and the next. Every day they met and every day he felt that particular brute strength and argued with her, and every day the little boy would come away feeling cross and powerless.

"Why did he keep going back to her?" you may ask.

Well he couldn't quite understand why, but he was intrigued by the way she played. She sang to herself, she gathered up the pebbles and chatted to them. She caught butterflies and whispered her secrets to them before she released them and laughed as they fluttered about her. It was as if all of nature loved being about this little girl. The sun always seemed to shine and sparkle on the water. The birds sang out their hearts to the trees, and the shy rabbits would edge to be near and nibble beside her as she played.

The little boy would watch her, wonder at the sound of her voice, and find himself smiling when she laughed. Deep inside, a part of him longed to laugh with her and

.....*he was intrigued by the way she played.*

26

play but something held him back: a paralysing fear of not knowing how to play, how to laugh, how to sing – and this fear felt very painful. It would make him sad, then angry and he would leap up and go over and start shouting at her.

Each day he would watch her for a little while longer before, consumed by his anger, leaping out and shouting at her. Each time he did this, he felt horrible and sick afterwards, not strong and powerful as he had expected to feel.

Finally on the fifth day he leapt out, lost his footing and fell headlong into the stream. His head hit a large round stone. As he lifted himself from the water, the pain began to overwhelm him. The girl watched the boy groping his way out of the stream in his wet clothes. With the throbbing pain spinning round his head, he was no longer able to hold on to the cross, disapproving expression on his face. The agony gushed tears out of his eyes and distorted his mouth which emitted a pitiful wail, a wail of such deep sadness and loneliness.

The sound of his distress brought the girl running over to him, where she gently placed her hand over the large lump that was appearing on the side of his head. The warmth from the little hand covering the wound spread pleasantly throughout his body and calmed his sobs. He was overcome by a great weariness. Heaviness closed his eyes and slowed his breathing, and he curled up on the bank of the stream beside the little girl and slipped into a gentle sleep.

She sat watching over him, singing quietly, waiting patiently while he had his deep rest and recovered.

After a while the boy woke up, the pain had left him. He looked up into the deepest, kindest eyes. Their beautiful warm glow enveloped his body, stretching deliciously he found himself grinning up at the little girl.

For the first time in his life he felt fully alive and happy, bursting with ideas, ideas for games that he could play with her, games of making rafts to float down the stream and little shelters for birds to build their nests in. Such energy surged through his body and filled his heart that he felt he would burst if he did not leap up and jump and shout – which he did. But this time he leapt for joy and shouted with laughter. It was the happiest day of his life.

The gentle hand of human kindness had touched him and he had been healed. No longer did he feel sad or angry. He now knew he could go back home with the knowledge that there was a wonderful world outside his parents' bitter home. A world that he was part of, a world where there was joy, kindness and sunshine; a world in which he would find friends, a world where he could be happy.

෴

"So what happened to him after that?" asked Sonya. "Did he carry on seeing the little girl?"

"Yes," said Willowby, "only for a short time though. You see she was a little gypsy girl, her family were travellers and they moved on somewhere else after a few days."

"Oh," sighed Sonya a little disappointed.

"Life for the little boy was different now, you understand," explained Willowby "The little gypsy girl had healed him with her kindness. He had only ever known unkindness, so he behaved unkindly when he met the little girl. He was afraid of other adults because he believed that all humans were unkind. That had been his only experience, so that was his reality – but even though it was normal for him, it didn't make him happy."

"But if he was so unhappy, how come he changed so quickly after the bump on his head? It doesn't make sense to change so easily."

"Ah," said Willowby, "that is the magic of kindness. It's called loving kindness. It has the power to change people for ever. It has the power to change their thoughts and their feelings and therefore their whole lives."

"So did the little boy's life change very much after that?" asked Sonya.

"Oh yes," replied Willowby. "The young boy grew up happy and strong, and all of nature responded to his happy feelings. When he met other humans, they responded to his happy feelings too and wanted to be his friend. One day he met a girl who reminded him very much of the little girl in the woods. He married her, and they were happy and they had children, and they were happy, and their children had children who were happy. So you see, the chain of unhappiness was broken for ever."

"What about the boy's parents? Did they change?"

"Things were a little better at home after that. The boy was so happy that he had discovered happiness that he felt sorry for his parents always feeling so cross all the time. He was patient with them and tried to be kind to them, and gradually they mellowed a little in their old age."

"Didn't he feel bitter about his unhappy life with his parents before he met the little gypsy girl?"

"Not at all, he was grateful for the experience of his sad early life, because now he could appreciate the happiness he had discovered all the more, because he knew from his own experience what it was like to live without happiness."

"What a wonderful story," said Sonya. "Was it true? Did it really happen? How do you know the story?"

"Yes it's true alright; just ask the pebbles in this brook, they remember. Besides, my mother saw it all, she used to grow just here, next to me. Of course water observes everything as it flows, carrying the news on its journey downstream. But the stones hold the memories."

Sonya thought of the little gypsy girl, how she had played just where she was now sitting. She looked down into the clear water bubbling over the shiny pebbles. Like the little girl before her she reached down and felt the smooth round surface of the jet black stone that beckoned to her. She marvelled at its mysterious dark lustre and its cool heaviness weighing in her hand.

Connected through time and place and the friendship of generations, a peaceful calm descended on the glade and the two friends as they contemplated all that had been said that day.

"You see," said Willowby after a while, "life is full of patterns, and these patterns are formed by people's actions, which are influenced by people's thoughts, people's feelings and people's reactions."

"Oh I think I see," replied Sonya. "The boy's life changed because the little girl was kind to him. Her kindness towards him created a new pattern."

"Why yes that's it!" replied the willow tree pleased. "Now we're getting somewhere." He smiled to himself and stretched, rippling his branches in approval as they danced around him to a rhythm all their own.

Deep in thought Sonya watched the dance of the tree and the patterns the gentle branches created as they swung in harmony together. In the distance the soft chorus of crickets joined in, as dusk began to creep up on the old tree and his young friend.

☙

THIRD INSIGHT
Nature is our Greatest Teacher
~

The Girl, the Groom and the Pony

"WHATEVER YOU DO in life will come back to you." said Willowby.

It was the following week and the middle of a heatwave. Sonya was talking to Willowby, secretly hoping for another story. The words he spoke hung peacefully in the air, as though everything in the wood was holding its breath, absorbing every sound Willowby uttered. All was silent, except for the gentle, rhythmic lapping of the water rippling over the pebbles as it flowed by.

"You know Sonya; life will provide us with all sorts of challenges to help us grow and develop. These challenges are simply lessons that can provide us with an opportunity to change our thoughts so that we become wiser. We can choose either to learn from them or ignore them."

"I don't understand," Sonya responded as she gazed upwards, eyes closed against the strong rays of sunlight that were beating down on the two friends that afternoon.

"Come into my shade and lie down; all this difficult thinking will give you a headache." Sonya did as he suggested and lay down, feeling the soft coolness of the turf beneath her back. She found herself looking up through the mystery of the branches to catch glimpses of the blue sky beyond. The summer's drowsiness defeated her and she drifted into the story that Willowby was now beginning to tell.

The Girl, the Groom and the Pony

THERE WAS A GIRL who had everything in life one could wish for: beautiful clothes, an enormous mansion with magnificent gardens, and servants to tend her every wish. She was very pretty and very bright, but she was very, very lonely.

Although she was rich, she was an orphan; she had no parents, and no brothers or sisters to play with. Her mother had died giving birth to her and her father had died of grief soon after. So she had never known her parents. There was an uncle who was her guardian and who managed the estates, but he was usually away at war or out hunting so she hardly ever saw him. This suited them both, as he was a cruel man and very ambitious. He resented the fact that his niece had inherited the great mansion and all the land. She had no friends in the world, not even animal friends. You see, rather like her uncle, she treated people badly.

She would find fault with the work of her servants, find any excuse to tell them off. She could be so unpleasant to them that, if they heard her coming down the corridor, they would run away and hide. When they were summoned into her presence to bring her meals, they would lay the food in front of her in silence, avoid eye contact and escape out of her presence as quickly as possible, and sigh with relief. They counted themselves lucky if they managed to do any job without being scolded.

When she went out into the garden, the ants would scurry away to hide deep in the ground when they heard her footsteps. The birds would flee any tree she walked near, cats would turn their backs and flick their tails at her in disdain if she passed by them, and the guard dogs would slink away and cower if they could smell her approaching. It seemed that all of nature felt uncomfortable in her presence.

Duchess, for that was this girl's name, had one great passion: riding. She loved to ride and she had ambitions to be the best rider in the country. She had seen her uncle and his friends ride. They always looked magnificent mounted on their steeds, so commanding that she wanted to be like them. One day she bought herself a pretty white pony, which she had seen performing beautifully on a neighbouring estate. She also arranged for the pony's groom to come, so that the pony would settle in and be properly looked after in his new home.

When the pony arrived, she couldn't wait to mount him and ride him. The groom, a gentle lad with kind dark eyes and a friendly smile, led the pony out to her. There was a happy spring in the pony's stride, he arched his neck and sent his poise flowing beautifully from the tip of his muzzle to the final flick of his tail. He enjoyed being on show, knowing he was admired by his new owner. As the boy and the pony waited for their instructions; the pony nuzzled the boy affectionately with his head, and the boy acknowledged his friend by fondly patting the pony's neck.

Duchess approached and the pony stood rock still, rigid, a glint of unease in his eyes. Duchess reached to stroke the pony's head, the pony tossed it up out of reach; she moved in alongside him to mount, and he backed away. The lad intervened talking sternly to the pony. The pony obeyed and allowed Duchess to mount him. The pony's whole body stiffened, his ears went flat back, he wrenched his head up and he side-stepped with discomfort.

Duchess cracked her whip and kicked her heels hard into the pony and they skedaddled off clumsily together. Gone was the happy spring in the trot and the flow to the tip of the tail. Duchess drove him towards a hedge. Pony swerved and lurched off in another direction. Duchess pulled him round, and pitched in again and launched him at the hedge a second time. Pony refused. A battle of wills was now declared between them, his against hers.

She kicked him and whipped him and shouted at him. He flared his nostrils, flattened his ears, lowered his neck and stuck his hooves deep in the ground. She screamed aloud at him, whipped in fury, and he reeled around and galloped away in outrage. He made for the trees, hoping a low bough would knock her off his back, but she ducked and clung to him, digging her nails deep into his neck. He veered off in desperation in the direction of a brook. Descending on it as fast as he could, he stopped dead, neatly depositing her on her head, in the deepest part of the running water. Triumphant in his new found freedom, he tossed his head, kicked his hooves in her direction and cantered away. The spring of joy in his stride, he whinnied with delight and recognition as he returned to his master.

"Alright, I see," the boy responded, patting the pony reassuringly on his neck. "That's how it is, is it? Well I'd better go and sort her out." He had gathered the whole

The spring of joy in his stride, he whinnied with delight and recognition as he returned to his master.

story, and walked off in the direction of the brook, leaving the pony alone to graze and recover his equilibrium. He found the girl wet, bedraggled, and bursting with rage, stomping away from the brook. As soon as she saw him, she vented all her fury and frustration on him.

"How dare you allow that pony to behave in such a way with me. He is way out of control and it is entirely your fault. He is totally unfit to ride, how dare you have the nerve to stand by and let me mount such a wild and dangerous fiend. I'll make you pay for this, the pair of you."

Sure enough, the next day, the boy and his pony were banished from the estate. They had to go and live on the scrubland beyond the walls, where there was no shelter and where they had to fend for themselves to survive. When the servants at the mansion heard of the boy's dismissal, there was great unease and unhappiness. They all knew him to be good, honest and gentle, and that he had to leave as a result of the anger of spoilt, unfriendly Duchess.

Now when Duchess strode around the estate, the dogs growled when she came near, the cats hissed, the bees refused to make honey and the birds fell silent. Servants huddled in corners as they whispered and plotted. Then one night, the guard unlocked the gate and gestured in a band of masked horsemen. The owl hooted their arrival, the dogs awoke and were alert but held silent. Someone led the masked men to the living quarters where, unaware that their lives were about to change for ever, Duchess and her uncle were fast asleep. They were swiftly bundled out of the mansion under the wraps of darkness, spirited away from the estate forever. No one ever knew what became of the uncle, but Duchess was abandoned in the scrubland in the belief that she would surely die.

The sunshine returned to the estate, the birds sang out their hearts again, mice played with the cats, dogs slept, flowers bloomed, all was well once more, and people sang as they went about their work.

Cold and alone, discarded in the scrubland, Duchess struggled with all her will to survive. Never ever having had to lift a finger to fend for herself, she managed very poorly now that she was alone. When she hunted, every animal ran from her, refusing to sacrifice one soul to her well-being. When she attempted fishing, no fish would surrender to her hook. Fruit ripened stubbornly on the branches, high up out of reach, and the trees made themselves inhospitable to her efforts to climb them and find safety among their boughs.

At night she retreated to the damp crevices of an abandoned burnt out oak, and as the days went by she grew weaker. Late one evening, in her wanderings, she came across a neat little wooden cabin. The door was open; someone obviously lived there but there was nobody to be seen. She went in; it was homely and inviting. There was a fire in one corner with a pot of simmering soup hanging above it. To the side, warmed by the heat of the fire, was a mattress stuffed with straw.

Duchess, so very hungry and tired, could not resist helping herself to the soup, and the soft straw mattress beckoned to her weary head and limbs. Her deep sleep was eventually broken by the sound of someone gently moving about the hut. Duchess lay there for quite a while, gradually coming to. Feeling as if she had finally emerged from a long and painful dream, she found enormous comfort in the gentle sounds of a person quietly going about their chores, and lay there basking in the new born feeling of safety that was growing within her.

She counted the songs of the birds as one by one they joined the chorus to celebrate the arrival of the new dawn.

Stretching and inhaling the cool air of this fresh morning, its vitality flowed through her veins, wakening the depth of her being. For the first time ever, she felt excited at the idea of waking and discovering the adventures that life had in store for her that day. She got up in search of the gentle mover who had woken her. The door to the outside world was ajar and she stepped out into the open air.

Imagine her astonishment at the sight of her former stable boy, brushing down the coat of the pony. Happy in each other's company, the boy was telling the pony how beautiful he was and the pony responded by nuzzling him with his head.

Duchess was overwhelmed by her feelings of remorse, a wail of anguish stuck in her throat unsounded. The shock of these two beings, in harmony together, made her lungs heave. The two, immediately aware that they were no longer alone, turned to greet their visitor.

She did not see the friendly smile that greeted her; her hands were covering her face in shame. Eventually curiosity took its lead and, sensing that all would be well, she gradually let her hands fall and lifted her head in his direction. She looked across at him and smiled shyly.
"How are you feeling? You were in such a deep sleep, I thought it better to leave you be." Then he added softly, "I've heard what has happened. I'm sorry."

With a shock she began to remember her former life; it seemed so long ago, so painful. This bright fresh morning heralded the start of a new life, bringing with it a feeling of happiness and well-being that she had never before experienced.

"Thank you," she said, and then confessed, "I helped myself to some soup, you know."

"There's plenty more," he laughed. "Come and make friends with Pony." Pony turned his head and challenged her with the steady gaze of his huge brown eyes. Greatly humbled she approached the pony. "Here, give him this," and the boy pressed a carrot into her hand.

She presented the peace offering to Pony, and Pony with the greatest delicacy took it from her outstretched palm. He munched it and the pleasure rippled along his back. She instinctively reached out and stroked his head; in return he nuzzled against her. They had become firm friends.

She took his brush from the boy and began to rub down his coat, telling the pony how beautiful he was. The sun rose greeting the three friends, the birds sang out the news to the world, and all of nature hummed in harmony. Peace had been declared, Duchess had found happiness and all the world responded.

She lived out her days in the scrubland, which became fertile and abundant with the fruit and crops she cultivated. At the turn of the seasons, she would take her produce to the large estate which had once been her home. She would walk through the gates which would close behind her, imprisoning her in her past domain. But she no longer belonged there, she walked unseen, no one greeted her, she was invisible to them. They didn't recognise the transformed child. Alas, they were blind to her. You see they toiled and toiled, enslaved by a new master. For the time being, their eyes were veiled from the new life that lay beyond their walls and which greeted them in their garden at the turn of each season.

❧

A hush had descended on the wood; every atom of life was deep in thought. Sonya lay there oblivious to the passage of the late afternoon sun, now lengthening its shadows across the glade. She was contemplating the voyage of discovery that Duchess had undergone, then, "So even the animals were unfriendly because she was."

"Yes," said Willowby, "they were showing her what it was like to be unfriendly."

"But even the fruit that ripened grew out of her reach."

"Yes," said Willowby again, "nature was demonstrating to her what she needed to learn about herself."

"So when she was so unfair to Pony and the groom,

her servants then plotted against her to remove her." Sonya was trying to think it through.

"Yes," confirmed Willowby. "Everything in her world conspired to teach Duchess the lessons she needed to learn."

"What exactly made her change? I don't think she would have changed if she had remained living in the big mansion."

"No, no," agreed Willowby, "Life had to get very hard for her, to break down her old ways of thinking and behaving. In the end she was too weak to resist change."

"She seemed to change after she ate the soup and after she slept on the warm mattress," declared Sonya.

"Oh yes," replied Willowby, "after her hardships she really appreciated the wholesome soup and the soft, warm mattress. Even though she had once lived in a beautiful mansion with magnificent gardens, she was happier living in a simple hut in the scrubland, because she was happier inside herself. Of course, every time she visited the estate with her produce, she would be reminded of her former sad life, and she would rejoice that she had found true happiness and abundance."

"But what I don't understand," queried Sonya, "is, why was she invisible to the workers on the estate? Why didn't they recognise her, or notice the difference in the scrubland?"

"They weren't looking for change; perhaps they were afraid of the world outside the safe, protecting walls of the estate. You see, life will present numerous clues or signs for you to notice, but the choice, my dear," and here Willowby lowered his tone to barely a whisper as his leaves swayed, "is yours. When you want change deep down inside yourself, nature will conspire to turn

40

life upside down to bring about that change within you."

"So Duchess really must have wanted change?"

"Oh yes," replied Willowby. "Remember she was very, very lonely. She had no friends, not even animal friends."

"So the pony came to teach her a lesson!"

"Exactly," affirmed Willowby.

"So you could say that the pony was her teacher."

"Indeed you could," rejoined Willowby delighted with the progress Sonya was making.

Sonya felt exhilarated. She leaped to her feet, feeling grown up and powerful with all her new knowledge. Suddenly, gripped by pangs of hunger for her mother's cooking, she declared, "I'm starving Willowby, I'm sure it's time for tea. Can we talk again tomorrow?"

"By all means," replied Willowby, "I'm hardly going to walk away, am I?" And all his leaves and branches began to shake and rustle with laughter.

"No, but ..." Sonya tried to explain helplessly, she felt really confused. "I so enjoy your stories and I still want to talk with you. You will be here to ..."

"Yes," pronounced Willowby, immediately solemn, his great solid stature bearing down on her, emphasising his stewardship of her.

Sonya went home, happy that there was still plenty more learning to enjoy with Willowby. She skipped towards the garden, and turned and waved before closing the little gate behind her. The great old willow swayed in reply."

❧

FOURTH INSIGHT
Life is a Mirror

❧

Crabface

THE NEXT DAY Sonya could not wait to visit the willow tree; she wanted to learn more. She could hardly keep the excitement inside herself as she thought of all the things she had learned from her friend. As soon as school was finished, she raced back home as fast as she could.

"Hello Willowby, I'm back," she called running up to him.

"Hello Sonya," Willowby replied, "and what's up with you today?"

"Oh everything, I'm really happy to be back here with you again." And she skipped around Willowby, tugging playfully at some of his branches as she wove in and around them.

Feeling the pleasure of her joy, Willowby studied her dancing with his branches, and waited for the time when she would share her happy thoughts with him.

After a short while the dance came to an end, and she stopped and looked up at him expectantly.

Willowby responded "Now, let me guess. Are you, by any chance, waiting for your next insight?"

"Oh yes Willowby I am," Sonya replied excitedly.

"Alright, let's begin," chuckled Willowby.

Sonya was all ears. Even the busy brook tiptoed by

so as not to miss a word of what Willowby was going to say.

"Life is a reflection of ourselves," he began, and looked at Sonya expectantly.

Feeling a response was in order, Sonya asked, "What do you mean by that?"

"Life is like a mirror, it's a reflection of ourselves. It reflects back at us what we feel inside."

"Oh," gasped Sonya, her eyes widening as an idea dawned on her, "Is that a bit like what happened to me at school today?"

Willowby peered closely at her, "Tell me, what did happen to you at school today?"

"Well I did something today just to try out one of the insights. You see, I've been thinking such a lot about the stories you've told me. Especially about how different life can be if you're happy. I kept thinking of Duchess and the Pony, how he disliked her when she was cruel and how they made friends when she gave him the carrot. So, I've been trying out being a nice duchess at school and seeing how people respond. And it works! It's just like magic."

Crabface

"THERE'S A TEACHER at school called Miss Crabbe, we call her Crabface because she's so cross and always seems to be in a bad mood. In fact, I'd been thinking about her since the story of the boy in the wood, I've been wondering if she is unhappy at home.

"Anyway, nobody in the class likes her because she never smiles and is always scolding us. Well, I thought I'd try being nice to her, like the little girl by the stream, to see if I could do any magic to make her smile and feel happy.

" ..... *she thanked me and said the flowers were lovely...*"

"We have her for geography first lesson after lunch. So, during the lunch break, I went up to the playing field to pick some daisies. I gathered a bunch and made some of them into a daisy chain, and then I picked some leaves to make a neat little posy. I felt so pleased because it looked so pretty. Anyway, I took them with me to class, and there was Miss Crabbe with her crabby face, all scowls as usual.

"She told us to wait outside the classroom until she was ready to let us in, and suddenly I felt scared of giving her the flowers. But then I kept thinking of Duchess and the little gypsy girl, except I didn't know when to give them to her. In the end, I just took a deep breath and knocked on the classroom door and asked if I could come in and

44

have a word with her. I didn't want to give her the flowers in front of the class in case they teased me.

"Anyway, Miss Crabbe told me to hurry up with what I wanted so I just held out the posy and chain and said, 'Miss Crabbe, I made these for you at lunch time, I hope you like them.' Then I tried to give her a big friendly smile.

"Oh you ought to have seen the expression on her face!" Sonya began to skip up and down, "She blushed, I've never seen her blush, and she smiled. Her eyes went all sparkly and wet. She looked quite pretty! Then she thanked me and said the flowers were lovely and that it was a very kind thought. She got up, filled a little jar with water to stand them in, and placed it on her desk. Then she thanked me again and said they brightened up the whole room. She gave me a big smile, and I suddenly realised she was a nice person.

"The change in her was dramatic; it was like magic, as if an ugly spell had been broken. She even made a few jokes and laughed when the class laughed. The lesson went really quickly for a change, and she announced that she would be letting us all off homework because we had worked so well. When we filed passed her at the end of the lesson, I gave her a big smile again and she smiled straight back, just like a friend.

"After the lesson the whole class was buzzing about the change in her. Some thought she'd fallen in love, and they tried to guess who it might be. Then they asked me if I'd said anything in particular when I was alone with her. So I confessed and said that I had given her a bunch of daisies as a present.

"'To her? Why? Why her?' They were all incredulous.
"'Well,' I tried to explain, 'she always looks so unhappy, so I thought I would try and cheer her up. I decided to pick

her a bunch of flowers, and you see it worked. It made her feel better, so she was nicer to us and we all benefited. Now,' I said, 'she's in such a good humour that she let us off our homework. So, you all owe me a favour.'" Sonya looked up at Willowby as she finished her story.

∾

"Go on," said Willowby.

"Well they seemed to accept what I said, and I felt a bit like a teacher, telling them what you had told me. I've been bursting to tell you. It felt so powerful doing this magic and yet it was so simple to do, and the result was totally amazing."

"Oh yes," agreed Willowby. "Now you know that you have the power within you to change the whole world around you, and everybody in it. Life is a reflection of you. Your feelings even transform the way you look, just as your crabface teacher smiled and looked almost pretty when your kind gesture made her feel happy."

Sonya fell silent and thought about this deeply. Willowby continued, gently yet with a sense of urgency, "Look out for life, my dear, it is full of surprises. People will often reflect yourself back to you; they will mirror how you feel. So be careful, look out for your feelings. Always remember, deep inside, you have the power to create any situation in your life. It is entirely up to you."

Sonya looked up at the sky as she thought to herself, "It's my choice, I have the power to create my own life; it's up to me. Nature will guide me because life will always reflect back exactly how I feel." She knew that this was true, and suddenly realised how lucky she was to have a best friend like Willowby.

FIFTH INSIGHT

Communication

❧

The Valley the Sun Forgot

FEW DAYS LATER, Sonya was sitting in her bedroom and Willowby's words echoed in her mind. "Look out for life, my dear, it is full of surprises. People will often reflect yourself back to you; they will mirror how you feel. So be careful, look out for your feelings. Always remember, deep inside, you have the power to create any situation in your life. It is entirely up to you."

"I wonder if that's true," she pondered. Just then she noticed the state of her bedroom, books flung all over the floor, dirty clothes heaped into a pile in a corner. The sight of the mess irritated her and she declared, "I can't be bothered to tidy up. It's just too boring; anyway, it'll take too long."

At that moment her bedroom door burst open and her little brother Jack charged into her room. A bomber jet bent on destruction, he zoomed round her homing in on his target. Trying to ignore him, Sonya turned to her dressing table mirror, picked up her hairbrush and started to brush her hair. Zooming up behind her, Jack exploded into a mass of ugly faces at her reflection.

Sonya slammed down the hairbrush and, turning on her brother, shouted, "Out!" and proceeded to push and bundle him out of the room. Her brother squealed, "Ow, you're hurting me, ow, let go!" Sonya shoved the door shut against him. Banging on it with his fists, he yelled, "What's the matter with you, Sonya? You hurt me. Mummy!" and raced downstairs to find her.

Satisfied that her young brother wouldn't dare to come near her for a while, Sonya sighed with relief and looked around. Noticing a blackbird pecking at the grass, she wandered over to the window, thinking, "I wonder what else I will learn today."

As if in answer to her question, the bird looked up and glinted one of its golden eyes directly at her. She suddenly felt very exposed and a feeling of shame over-whelmed her. She backed away from the window, returned to the safety of her dressing table, and picked up her brush. Drawing comfort from the familiar object, she found solace in the rhythmical routine of brushing her hair.

She contemplated her reflection in the mirror. Her heart paused for a moment and almost missed a beat as she caught a glimpse of the blackbird flying across the garden into the wood and alighting on one of Willowby's branches. Her mind began to race, "Whatever is the bird telling Willowby?"

No time for a reply, she was shocked out of her thoughts by her door suddenly opening to reveal her mother standing in the doorway. Her practised eye swept the untidy bedroom, taking in the heap of clothes in the corner and the books strewn across the floor, before finally resting on Sonya's reflection.

Caught in her gaze, Sonya knew she couldn't escape the telling off she knew was coming.

"You're room is a pigsty. You're not going anywhere until it's tidy, do you hear?"

Sonya glowered in response. It was all her brother's fault. Her mother turned to go, ignoring Sonya's angry glares, then added, "When you have finished tidying your room, you can come and help me in the kitchen," before closing the door behind her.

Alone in her room once more, Sonya slammed down her brush in fury and mimicked her mother to the mirror, "'First tidy your room, then help in the kitchen.' What a boring day, why can't I go and see Willowby?" She gazed mournfully at the reflection of the passing clouds in the sky and drifted over to the window again. Willowby's leaves were waving in the wind. Was he beckoning to her? Perhaps if she just chucked her clothes in the wardrobe and shoved her books under the bed, no one would know. She could always sort them out properly later. That way she could get out and chat with Willowby.

Inspired by the brilliance of her plan, she quickly set to work and cleared away the clothes and books, silently chuckling to herself, no one would ever notice, she was so clever. She could just imagine her mother's surprise if she happened to enter the room. Satisfied, Sonya softly clapped her hands as her foot nudged the last book out of sight under the bed.

Creeping down the stairs, she paused, hearing her mother's voice on the telephone. Stealthily, she put on her shoes, opened the back door and ran across the lawn to the gate and hurried through the trees towards the small glade where she could see Willowby waiting for her.

Rushing up to him, she tugged one of his branches, calling out in delight, "You see, Willowby, I made it!"

Willowby looked down at her surprised. He had not

been expecting her and she had roused him from a short nap he was taking.

"Hello, Sonya, you're rather early aren't you?" he remarked in a sleepy voice. "Are you sure you're supposed to be out? Isn't there something else you should be getting on with right now?"

"Oh, it isn't important Willowby, I wanted to talk with you again and I couldn't wait. I can do my chores later," replied Sonya as she hung on his branches, leaning back and gazing up into his kind old face.

"Indeed. Is that so?" And he fixed her with a penetrating stare.

Sonya suddenly felt guilty. "But you were beckoning to me to come out," she protested.

"I was?"

"Oh yes, your leaves were waving to me through the window."

"They were?" Willowby's voice deepened sharply as Sonya continued.

"Yes they were, I could see them, and this blackbird flew onto your branches and was talking to you."

"Ah."

"And I wanted to know what he'd told you."

"Now we have it at last, the real reason." Willowby chuckled loudly rattling his leaves with mirth, observing Sonya squirming with discomfort.

She looked up at the figure of Willowby rocking backwards and forwards in laughter, then dropped her head and covered her face in shame as she thought of the incident with her mother. She suddenly felt sick inside as she remembered what she had done to her brother, and how she had not tidied her room properly.

Willowby felt the confusion she was suffering as

the realisation of her words and actions hit her. He immediately stopped laughing and stroked her tenderly with one of his branches. Sonya dared to look up at him again. The distress in her eyes was met by an expression of deep understanding and kindness.

"You know it's much healthier to recognise the truth and say it. Your body knows what is true, and yearns to communicate it," Willowby explained patiently. "You see, people become aware of the truth anyway, without you having to speak it. Somehow, eventually, you or your body will find a way of revealing the truth, whether you want to or not." Sonya glanced away, and Willowby looked down at her and continued gently. "It's an effort swallowing the truth all the time; it's much better to have the courage to speak the truth right from the start. You'll feel lighter because, you see, speaking the truth sets you free."

Sonya raised her head slowly and looked into the depths of Willowby's ancient eyes. He nodded in acknowledgement. At that moment a sharp breeze rushed passed carrying a flock of birds who were ducking and diving and calling out with glee. Sonya gazed up at them as they soared into the heavens, free. She could feel how wonderful it would be to be as light and free as a bird. She blushed and looked sheepishly down towards her hands that were busily clasping and unclasping.

"Tell me," Willowby encouraged her gently.

Sonya took a deep breath and began, "Well, Willowby, this morning I shouted at my brother and then I was rude to my mother, and I didn't tidy up my bedroom."

"Why not?" asked Willowby.

"I didn't feel like it and I didn't see why I should!"

51

"Why not?" Willowby repeated.

"Well, I couldn't be bothered, I felt awful inside and I wanted to see you," she retorted. Sneaking a sideways glance up at the tree, she caught sight of the surprised look on his face.

"Anyway," she gushed defiantly, "what's the point of tidying up a room when the next minute it's all messy again?" Sonya shrugged her shoulders, shuffled from one foot to the other and tossed her head in defiance.

"Well Sonya," replied Willowby in his deep, gentle tone, "it is a good idea to keep your room tidy; a well ordered environment is a reflection of a well ordered mind. So if you tidy your room, it helps to discipline your mind. Remember, the thoughts in your mind, whether or not you are aware of them, have the power to shape your life."

Sonya looked up into Willowby's kind old eyes, as the wisdom of his words sunk in. She smiled to herself, she totally trusted him. "Alright Willowby," she replied after some thought, "if what you say is true, then, in future, I will try to keep my room tidy, and if that helps me in my life then great!"

There, she'd said it. Sonya looked up at the birds to catch their reaction; they swooped down and called out in response to her. "How exciting," she thought, "they understand!" At that moment, for the first time, she felt connected to the power of the whole universe. Immediately feeling lighter, she now realised that, with its help, she could achieve anything. At this, she looked directly at Willowby and grinned broadly.

Willowby responded by declaring, "I think you're ready for the next insight now," Sonya looked at him expectantly. "Yes," continued Willowby, "I think it's vital that you understand the laws of communication."

"Communication?" replied Sonya, "What do you mean by communication?"

"Communication happens when messages are sent and received by someone or something. These messages are conveyed in different ways, either through the language of sound, that is speech or music, or through the language of silence wherein lie the languages of the body, the mind and feeling."

Again the sharp breeze rustled up and Willowby's leaves shook violently. The birds high in the sky cried out. "Oh yes," chuckled Willowby. "Have patience, I haven't finished yet," and he went on. "Of course there are thousands of languages to learn, languages of all the species within the animal kingdom, the plant world, and the mineral world, and the languages of all the other universes. They all communicate with each other and with us. It's simply a matter of learning the language. Oh yes," continued Willowby seriously, "to learn the mode of communication is indeed the most important of all the insights for you to understand. You see, true communication leads to joy and harmony. True freedom resides in a universe of joy and harmony."

Sonya had received her cue; she was already nestled beside Willowby's roots, waiting for him to begin....

The Valley the Sun Forgot

ONCE UPON A TIME a long time ago there was a town which was lodged in the valley of an imposing mountain. The town was always in shadow; the sun hadn't visited the valley for hundreds of years so no vegetation grew there and a dark cloud hung low over it always.

It was as if all the people of the town permanently carried this cloud on their shoulders, and they felt the burden of it continually as they went about their work.

They all walked with a stoop, looking down at the ground; they rarely looked up to communicate with the cloud that hung above them – what was the point? It had always been there, it never changed and it would most likely be there for ever. Such was the dull law that ruled their dull lives.

Because the sun never visited the valley and nothing grew, there were no crops. So most people worked long hours in the depths of the mountain, extracting stones and boulders which they set on trucks that were carted away to build cities and palaces in far off lands. Few strangers ever passed that way, which was just as well; they would have received a cold welcome. Not that the people were deliberately unfriendly, you understand, but they appeared dark and hostile and inhospitable, like the mountain that towered over them. You see, the people rarely talked to each other; they certainly did not tell jokes or entertain each other with songs or stories. Communication was limited almost entirely to task-related conversation. Their language sounded harsh, clipped and impatient. There was no word for holiday in the language of this valley; there had never been a day free from toil. The people worked long hours every single day of their short lives.

Darkest and most silent of all in that town was Jerome the Blacksmith. Angry that life had taken away his wife at a young age and had left him with no son, Jerome stoked and stoked his furnaces to greater heats and forged heavier and sharper tools; weapons that were famous for wielding their strength against the rocks and boulders in the heart of the great mountain. The sound of the smithy could be heard all day, and often all night, as Jerome battled and worked to repair tools for the new onslaught that the following day would bring.

Jerome lived alone but for his daughter. Cruelly disappointed that he had no son to train into his business, he had taught his daughter the skills of forging metal, but her efforts always failed to please him. Her work was delicate and light to the touch, surprisingly strong and exquisite to handle. However her father despaired of her ever being able to produce tools and weapons of sufficient weight and force to be used against the rocks of the mountain. What would become of his business? Aurora felt the burden of his disappointment as he scolded her over the furnaces late into the night.

"What will become of you? This tool is not fit to wield against even the smallest stones within Mount Doomid."

Nevertheless Aurora worked at her craft undaunted. When she was done with her day's chores, she was wont to gaze into the glowing coals of the furnace and smile secretly, as if the fire itself communicated with her and taught her how to fashion the metals to her style.

The metals she and her father used came from Mount Doomid and carried Doomid's character: dark, heavy and coarse. It was indeed extraordinary, therefore, that Aurora succeeded in forging objects of such exquisite finesse. Any outsider would have marvelled at such work, but there never was an outsider passing by to acknowledge her talent. Her father regarded the fruits of her toil as worthless and refused to pay her, and she was forced to spend her days working in the mines cutting the rock out of the heart of the mountain.

This she did by day, and every evening she worked into the night with the furnace. She never complained but would smile mysteriously when she was alone with her fire and her metal, and every morning she would produce yet one more artefact of most exotic beauty.

One day Aurora was working deep inside Mount Doomid as usual, digging at stones. She was tired, her back ached and her hands were split and sore. Suddenly her pickaxe struck a rock of a completely alien quality. It sang out a sound of resounding harmony whenever she struck it, a sound harmonising pain, joy and mystery. She looked around expecting to see everybody else in the mine looking her way in astonishment. But nobody seemed to have heard the strange and beautiful sounds; they were all absorbed in the battle with the rock and the beating of boulders with ferocious force.

Aurora stooped and looked closely at the stone. She could tell it was some kind of metal ore, the like of which she had never seen before. It was smooth to touch, dark but with a light gleam. She prised and levered it until it came loose. When she lifted it up and set it on her cart, she was surprised to discover how light it was to carry. Fascinated, she resolved to take it home with her and work on it in the furnace that evening.

Sure enough, when evening came, she hurried home, prepared her father's meal and waited until he had dozed off in his chair before creeping out to the forge. When she entered, the furnace glowed menacingly at her. It had been hard at work all day sharpening tools in preparation for a new onslaught on Mount Doomid the following morning. Aurora knelt before the furnace and felt its heat burn into her cheeks. Closing her eyes, she breathed in the heat and felt it penetrate her tired limbs and spine.

After a few minutes she dragged herself back from the red-hot fire and went out to fetch the curious lump of ore she had found that afternoon. Returning with her precious find, she sat in front of the furnace, exploring the ore's surface with her fingers. As she sat absorbed by its smooth texture, she became aware that the fire had started to spit excitedly and shoot out hungry tongues of flame. She wondered what had disturbed the fire for it to behave so. Usually it glowed quietly, conserving its energy for action. Strange! She looked back at the lump of material in her hands and gasped in astonishment. The surface of the ore was glowing golden red, and the flames of the spitting furnace were creating patterns of darting wings deep within the ore.

Mesmerised by the heat and the fire and the power of the ore in her hands, Aurora found herself rolling the alluring lump of ore towards the furnace. She reached for the tongs and pushed it towards the hungry flames, which seemed to gasp and devour it. Grabbing her hammer and tools, she swiftly and expertly began to fashion it as the fire and ore together urged her.

Before her eyes the ore burned bright gold. Her tools had forged an extraordinary creature with fiery out-stretched wings, a neck which craned upwards away from its mortal body towards heaven. Its strong beak depicted an aristocratic curve of ancient lineage, and its head proudly bore a crown of strange and distant origin. Aurora gazed in awe at the creature she had forged. She allowed it to cool in front of her to a warm glinting gold.

Eventually she picked up the object. It was surpris-ingly light and felt silky smooth to the touch. She looked curiously at all the markings. The eyes were stern yet ancient and wise; the beak was closed as if the bird were sceptical and slightly haughty. She admired its proud neck, the exquisite structure of the enormously powerful wings. The figure stood about one foot tall, and was indeed the most intriguing object she had ever crafted. However when she looked into the eyes of this curious creature, she knew full well that she had actually had little to do with the creation of this remarkable piece of handiwork. How had it come to be? She could only gaze at her friend the furnace and contemplate the mystery and wonder at it all.

As she turned the figure over in her hands, a forceful power surged through her blood and she felt an urgent need to guard this figure with the utmost care. She heard her father stir behind her and realised it was gone midnight. She wrapped the curious bird in her apron and tucked it under her pillow before falling asleep. That night she dreamed that she rode on the back of a great golden bird that flew up and touched the rim of the sun. She dreamed that she flew beyond the sun to a galaxy of stars and planets far away, to a galaxy which pulsated with harmony and joy, where the planets floated in a universe of great beauty, where the plants sang to the people, and where the people bowed down to the plants and danced with the animals and sang with the birds. On the golden bird, she flew through the universe, landing on the planets, where they celebrated her arrival and treated her as a great Queen come from a far off land. She came away piled with gifts which she distributed amongst the passing stars until finally returning home she woke with a start. Lying there astonished at her dream, she was aware that she was still carrying, within her, one remaining gift: this gift was the beautiful light, which she felt glowing in her heart, a glow that made her smile and tempted laughter from her lips. Every time she laughed, she felt sunlight dance across her face. This tickled and made her laugh even louder. The sound awoke her father in alarm, and Aurora curled up hugging her joy to herself for safe-keeping. Suddenly panicking, her hand shot under her pillow to feel for her precious object, the object of the night before, the object of her dream – it was still there.

Aurora got up and bathed before setting off for work. The water felt particularly refreshing and gentle that morning. She yearned to sing out loud, but only permitted herself a soft hum. She found that when she sang, even ever so gently, her steps were lighter and she felt less weary, and she caught glimpses of the sun trying to shine his beams down to dance with her. Deep inside the mountain that day, Aurora got out her precious golden bird-like figure and placed it in front of her. It glowed with such a powerful light that it lit up every corner of the dark cavern. Sensing the mountain sigh with pleasure, she became aware that its breath was no longer bitingly cold and dank but sweet smelling and soft. Now when she inhaled, she felt the strength of the ancient mountain penetrate her bones.

Aurora carried the figure around with her every-where. When she admired its beauty, she saw it glow with pleasure at being appreciated. She was very conscious that the mountain delighted in its presence. So, everyday, just for a short time, she would bring the figure out and its luminescence would fill the heart of the mountain and the mountain would sigh sweetly.

When she unwrapped the figure during the day, the sun would find a way of peeping from behind the heavy cloud to catch a glimpse, and at night the moon would light up the heavens and the stars would draw near and sparkle brightly. What's more, it became apparent that when Aurora carried the figure in her apron pocket, her father scolded her hardly at all. At night in her dreams, with her precious bird safely under her pillow, she flew on the back of the golden creature to the far off lands of light and warmth where joy and harmony abounded.

A month quickly passed, and Aurora lived in private happiness with her secret companion. She marvelled at the changes around her that she was beginning to witness. Every time she awoke from her dreams, she couldn't stop herself thinking, "Why can't it be like that here? How can I bring joy to Doomak?" She began to behave as they did on other planets. Every time she saw the sun, she greeted it and laughed with delight as it responded by darting down a beam to her. At night she sang to the moon and the stars as they drew near, and she felt the comforting velvet of the night draw round to keep her safe until morning. Aurora, always brought up to be alone and always having felt very lonely, now began to realise that she was surrounded by friends with whom she could communicate.

But as the days passed, there grew an urgency within her and around her pressing for change in the world she knew. The time came when the moon was in her full-blown glory and Aurora sat crouched in front of the furnace, fingering her figurine. "Why can't our town be full of song and joy, like those other worlds in the universe?" she asked the figure as she traced his fine lines with her finger.

When all at once the phoenix, for that's what it was, let out a deafening roar and rose majestically out of the flaming fire.

61

As if in response, the bird became suddenly hot in her hands, too hot to handle. She dropped it, and to her horror it landed just at the edge of the furnace. The furnace began to spit and lash out its hungry flaming tongues towards the bird.

"No," cried Aurora, "you'll melt."

"Have faith," the flames flickered at her, "look what we made together a month ago. Do you really want to carry on living just with your dreams of a possible new world? Dare to push your friend towards us and be prepared to be amazed."

As if in a trance, Aurora did as she was bid and shoved the bird into the heart of the furnace. As she did so a prayer escaped from her heart via her lips, a prayer for a world of joy and harmony.

Instantly, in front of her, the furnace burst into life and she leapt back to safety. Hot wings of flame were fanning her and then the furnace reached up and towered over her, reaching for the heavens. She crouched in awe at what was happening, yet strangely felt no fear. She could not tear her eyes away from the furnace. She was intrigued at what she was witnessing. The wings took solid form, a proud neck craned towards her; a fearsome beak was reaching out to inspect her. When all at once the phoenix, for that's what it was, let out a deafening roar and rose majestically out of the flaming fire.

Aurora flung herself out of the way of the great bird, landed on her back, and found herself looking up at the most awesome spectacle. Perched on a broken wagon, the regal bird was checking out his brand new life body.

"Oh Ah Oooooh that's better," a distinguished voice crowed. "Free at last, at long last freedom." The voice heralded as the wings were stretched and the neck was flexed. "Oh it's been a long time this time round," he declared, hopping from one foot to the other, "freedom, freedom, freedom." He had obviously not hopped for a very long time, and on the last freedom he lost his balance and went crashing to the floor. "Oh my wings – too slow, too slow, ow, ow, ow, ow, ow."

Aurora, who'd been watching the transformation with utter amazement, suddenly began to laugh out loud at the spectacle of an exceedingly distinguished bird with such a regal head, hopping clumsily from one foot to the other before landing spread-eagled beside her.

The phoenix, with his dented pride, was not slow to rebuke her, "Laugh, laugh, you may do so, loud as you like, but imagine how you would feel if you'd been trapped underground for several hundred years in a lump of ore. Oh the freedom to be free, it's delicious!" and he stretched out each claw on his feet and hopped from one to the other in sheer delight, this time maintaining his balance till the end.

Aurora felt rather humbled when she heard this. "Oh I'm so sorry," she began, "I didn't mean to offend you…"

"Oh please don't apologise. Indeed I'm forgetting my manners. Goodness me, it's been so long since I spoke to anyone or felt my wings stretch. Beloved child, thank you for releasing me, thank you, thank you."

"Please, I don't feel I've done anything special," protested Aurora, "I am sure that it's the fire that is really responsible."

"Yes indeed to be sure," rejoined the phoenix, "but you brought me to the fire remember, on two occasions."

"I did?"

"Yes, yes surely you must remember." The phoenix reasoned with Aurora, "First you brought the lump of ore to the fire to create the image of me, then you threw me into the fire to bring me to life. It is you I need to thank, if it wasn't for you I would still be imprisoned in that lump of ore in the heart of Mount Doomid."

"Well I'm sure it was just a coincidence really, anybody could have found that boulder."

"Coincidence? Coincidence?" The phoenix looked as though he was going to take off he became so impassioned over the word.

"Yes," Aurora replied perplexed; she could not understand what had inflamed the phoenix so.

"Oh my young friend, coincidence, there is no such thing in the world as coincidence. No, no sweet one, you brought this about yourself. Of that there is no doubt." The phoenix leant towards Aurora to drive home his message. "Your thoughts and your dreams led you to me. And for that I am truly grateful. In fact, I would like to repay you in some way one day, if I may."

"You're very kind," replied Aurora, not knowing how else to respond to a phoenix so fearsome in his passion and to something she didn't really understand. She was intrigued. "What did he mean about there being no such thing as a coincidence? And what thoughts had led her to him?"

"Let me explain," answered the creature, obviously reading her mind. "You have been born with a talent for sculpting beauty out of base metal. You have persisted in creating objects of beauty despite the fact that you have only ever been scolded for your efforts. However, that will soon change. Your persistence in creating objects of beauty led you to find that precious lump of ore within

64

which I was imprisoned."

"That may well be," responded Aurora modestly, "but there is no way that I alone could have fashioned you into the beautiful image that you were, or indeed have transformed you into the living being that you are now."

"Just so," replied the phoenix. "However, in life, if you've carried a dream in your heart and if you have fulfilled your tasks to the best of your ability, there will come a time when magic will step in to make that dream come true."

"Magic?" Aurora's head began to reel, "Dreams? But what dreams, other than one of living in a different kind of world?" she asked mystified.

"Precisely, precisely," interrupted the phoenix in great excitement, hopping from foot to foot, flapping his wings. "Absolutely – it is precisely that dream which was needed to resurrect me. Once you became aware in your dreams that there are worlds where joy and harmony and peace exist, you then desired to have that here. So the magic to release me became possible. And so the fire, the great spirit of freedom, was bound to assist you. Most importantly, you were also prepared to sacrifice the image of me to realise the reality."

"I was?"

"Yes you were," the phoenix responded softly. "Do you remember dropping me by the fire and pushing me into the heart of the furnace?"

"Why yes," gasped Aurora, all of a sudden remembering her distress at the thought of the beautiful figurine melting before her eyes. The memory of the fire urging her on caught up with her and she fell silent. Eventually one burning question forced its way to the surface of her reflections: "What I don't understand, is how you came to be locked up in a lump of ore inside the mountain, in the first place."

"It's a long sad tale," sighed the phoenix. And for the first time the proud strong neck drooped and the brilliant glow of his golden feathers dimmed. "But I will tell you briefly." He paused, then took a deep breath before whispering, "It was a sort of curse."

"A curse?" exclaimed Aurora in alarm. "What happened?"

In painful, hushed tones the phoenix continued, "Once upon a time a very long time ago, this valley was just like a planet you visited with me in your dreams. Doomak was known by another name in those happy days: Luminaria, where animals lived in harmony with humans, without fear. They were not hunted for food, there was no need; humans knew how to cultivate beautiful crops, and the vegetation on the land took care of all their needs. They would dance for rain and sing for sun and mild weather, and the guardians of the planet responded. Everybody and everything lived in joy and harmony, and fear was not known.

"However, flying over the land one day, came the black eagles of the northern lands, who cast an envious eye over this happy valley. They had squandered their vegetation, and their country lay in tatters after years of war. They were flying in search of better lands to plunder. As they flew low over the country, they began to sow seeds of discontent, and the people of Luminaria began to look at each other and covet what others had. They began to neglect their dancing and singing, and they had no time to woo the vegetable kingdom to produce food. So when the crops began to fail them, they resorted to hunting the dear animals to satisfy their hunger. The wild animals fled in terror; those that remained were captured and imprisoned. The sun was so disgusted that she ceased to smile on the valley and the lands became barren. When food ran out, the people began tunnelling into Mount Lumini and digging out its heart in order to trade with the evil eagles of the northern lands.

"I'm Luminarto, the Great Spirit of the mountain, and I resided in its heart. My job was to roam freely, and over-light the valley with my spirit which is freedom. It was not meant that I should be trapped inside a body.

"Naturally, as the inhabitants turned their back on me and began to rip out the heart of the mountain, I knew I would not be able to survive. If I died, the valley would be lost forever. So I communed with the spirits of the North, the South, the West and the East and they created a great storm and wrapped me up in a thunder-bolt and fired me into the heart of the mountain. There I would remain until the time was ripe, until the time when the hands of a girl, pure in heart, would reach out towards me."

"But aren't you in danger now?" asked Aurora with some concern.

"No," said the phoenix stretching his proud neck and flexing his wings. "Times have changed; you have been dreaming of a better world, you have been communicating that dream to your environment. Everything is now primed and ready to support you."

"I don't understand. How have I been communicating with my environment?" Aurora was at a loss to under-stand what he meant; it sounded so serious, so formal, such a responsibility.

"Aurora my friend," Luminarto the phoenix commanded. "Think hard, it is not too long ago. Do you remember the tongues of fire? What did you do when the sun replied by sending her beams down to dance with you? Think of the breath of the mountain after you had created the image of me."

Aurora thought hard, and all the memories and sensations returned to her, and as she relived those memories she drew a sense of power and strength into her body.

The phoenix watched over his charge. "Splendid, splendid, now young one, it is time. We have great work to do over the next few weeks. But now you should take some rest."

"Work? What work?" Aurora asked, intrigued.

"Transformation."

"Transformation?"

"Yes, you want to change the valley, don't you?"

"Yes, but …"

"So we have work to do." Luminarto drew himself up to his full height and stamped both feet. "We'll start tomorrow."

"But how?" Aurora yawned; a great sleep was beginning to overpower her.

"Sleep Aurora, dream, dream, you will know. The ideas will come to you. Allow them to. Give them the time and the space, that is all. Sleep and dream. Sleep to dream." Luminarto's voice had reduced to the softest croon, and Aurora had drifted into the land of dreams.

That night a tree spirit visited Aurora in her dreams. The tree spirit offered to return to grow and give shelter and food, if the humans were prepared to help create a healthy land. It also informed Aurora that the spirits of

68

other vegetation were willing to return if the humans were ready to cooperate. The next day Aurora told the phoenix of her dream.

"Ah ha," replied Luminarto delighted, "that's a start. I will spread the dream to the other townsfolk."

So during the next seven nights the phoenix visited every inhabitant of the town, and all the people began to dream of a life where vegetation had returned to the valley. When they woke, they began to yearn for vegetation to return.

After seven days Aurora dreamed again; this time the spirit of the sun paid her a visit. The sun promised to return and smile down on the valley again and allow his sunbeams to play over the land to encourage the crops to grow and to lighten the hearts of the sad valley dwellers.

The next day Aurora informed Luminarto of her latest dream, and the phoenix spent the following seven nights spreading the dream of the return of the sun amongst the people of the shaded vale. And sure enough, when the townsfolk awoke they began to yearn for the sun. They looked up at the cloud and pleaded with it to lift and allow the sun to shine.

At the end of the second week Aurora dreamed that the spirits of the rocks and stones pleaded with her to be left alone in peace under the mountain. They complained that they had lost too many of their relations, they feared that none of them would survive if the plundering of the mountain continued. They explained to her that the mountain depended on their strength to survive, and that the surrounding valleys relied on the mountain because of its ability to touch the sky and absorb the celestial light which made its way down to them by way of the mountain streams.

And again Aurora told the phoenix of her dream, and again during the seven nights the phoenix flew amongst the inhabitants of the town and spread the dream. In a very short time, after waking from this latest dream, the folk began to resent going to the mines every day to work. As it so happened, just at this time, the low hanging grey cloud responded to the valley dwellers' prayers. It lifted itself high into the heavens to reveal a dazzling blue sky graced by a smiling, shining sun. The inhabitants were overjoyed, and a national holiday was immediately declared. People gazed up at the sky, and began to talk about it to each other and laugh, and one or two made up songs in celebration of the extraordinary event.

The next day dawned bright and blue again, and again a national holiday was agreed by all. The people began to dance and sing. Luminarto flew up to greet the sun and then shot like lightning into the heart of the mountain. The mountain mumbled and gurgled with delight to be reunited with its spirit, though it has to be said that the inhabitants, unfamiliar with the language of the mountain, became alarmed at its rumblings. Then and there they all decided that the mountain was too dangerous to enter again, and that from now onwards it was best to leave the mountain tunnels well alone.

By the end of three weeks, joy, happiness and harmony were fast returning to the valley. One or two people discovered bits of vegetation that were taking root, and tried eating it and found that it was good. There was still something missing however, but nobody could quite come up with what it was.

That night Aurora dreamed again. In this dream the spirit of the animals visited her. They were tired of living in exile, in constant fear of being hunted. They wanted to return as they had heard that the vegetation had returned and that the sun smiled on the valley again. But they wanted assurances that the inhabitants would not hunt them.

The next morning Aurora told the phoenix of her dream, and during the next seven nights Luminarto spread the dream of the spirit of the animals. The next few days, people began to wake and lose their appetite for needless hunting. What's more, people suddenly remembered what it was that was missing in their new found paradise, and began to long for the sound of birds in the air, the sight of butterflies in the sun, and the companionship of a dog or cat beside the hearth.

Luminarto flew south and communed with the animal kingdom, and gradually, species by species, the animal kingdom returned to Doomak the valley of Doomid.

One month had passed since their work had begun, and Luminarto worked every night and every day to bring about transformation in the valley. But he knew that in his present form he could not sustain the intensity of the work needed. The moon was full and the stars had drawn near as they had a month earlier.

Luminarto drew breath, "The time is ripe," he announced. "I must now take the final step towards full transformation, and you must help me. I need you to help me to release my spirit into the valley."

"Certainly I will help," replied Aurora, "but I'm not sure how. You must tell me exactly what you want me to do."

"It's quite simple," replied Luminarto, "but you may find it rather difficult."

"All you need to do is tell me," said Aurora, "and I'll gladly carry out your wishes."

Luminarto shook his head gravely, "My young friend, don't speak so readily about something of which you know very little. I know you will find this next step hard, but it is necessary. Listen carefully."

Aurora settled herself down at his feet and looked up into the distinguished features to which she had become so attached.

Luminarto began quietly and steadily. "This is what is going to happen." He looked directly ahead as he spoke. "I am going to stand before the furnace, then I will leap into the flames and I want you to push me into the heart of the furnace where it is hottest. This is most important – will you promise to do that for me?"

Horrified, Aurora cried out, "But you will burn, you will hurt, you will die. I cannot do it, I will never see you again. Don't ask me to do this, please don't."

"Please help me Aurora," Luminarto replied. "It is the only way to release my spirit. I am a spirit of fire. It takes fire to release me, but I cannot do this alone. I need your help."

"But why? Why me?"

"Because you are the guardian of my transformation; it was you who found me and created my image, it was you who created my being. Now it is you who needs to help me make this final transformation. It is your job. The valley is reawakening; I need once more to take on the role of over-lighting spirit. My spirit needs to be released over the land. I cannot do this work in a physical body."

"But I'll miss you. We've had such wonderful times together, we work so well together." Aurora sobbed, pleading with him.

The phoenix leaned over and tenderly stroked her head with an outstretched wing. "This part of our work is completed now, I must move on. I will still be around you; you will still be able to communicate with me, just as you are doing now. You will catch glimpses of me if you look into the flames, if you look up at the sun and if you do not run from lightning. You'll see, you will see me everywhere." He stepped away towards the fire and drew himself up to his full height. "Come my most trusted friend, the moon cannot delay her passage. Now is the time. Remember to push me into the heart of the heat. I will feel no pain. Thank you Aurora, thank you, thank you; do not fear."

Aurora cried out to her friend. He leaped.

The fire exploded before her, and the most beautiful singing rang out to the heavens. Then a great wind whistled around her and transported a winged flame high into the sky. As it passed she felt the touch of the lightest plumage caress her cheek. She looked up at the choir of stars above her. They were singing the harmonies of the universe, the sounds of true freedom.

Then there was stillness; the land was alive, awake and waiting. Aurora waited. She waited and watched until she saw the dawn break. As the sun stretched out his early beams over the mountaintop, she glimpsed Luminarto riding high above the rising, shining orb. As the sun rose higher he stretched out his wings towards her, and she felt his light on her eyelids and the warmth of his heat in her heart. She inhaled the breath of the new dawn, freedom. She understood now, and smiled at a job well done.

✖

Willowby stopped talking, and the powerful sound of silence prevailed over the glade in the wood. Here the two friends contemplated the ancient story that the little brook was now babbling out excitedly, as it pattered over the pebbles.

Eventually Sonya stretched, "So what happened to Aurora in the end, and did the valley really change?"

"Oh yes," replied Willowby. "It became a land of freedom. Because their lives had changed so much and they were now so happy, they decided to celebrate the valley's birthday by renaming it. The names Mount Doomid and the Valley of Doomak didn't suit the place at all and reminded them of the dark days. As it happened, a few of them had a dream one night and the next day they woke with the new name of the valley and mountain on their lips: Mount Lumini and the valley of Luminaria."

"Those were their names in the old, old days, before the dark set in," exclaimed Sonya.

"Quite right, you are quite right," agreed Willowby, who was impressed that his young friend had remembered the details of the story so clearly.

"And what about Aurora, what happened to her? Did she carry on working for her father?"

"Well she certainly continued to create exquisite objects with the furnace. People began to take notice of the beauty and extraordinary craftsmanship of her work. Her gardening tools were known to work as if by magic. Her fame grew far and wide, and people came to the valley to honour her work. Her craftwork always bore the stamp of a phoenix, and after she died the valley adopted the emblem of the phoenix out of respect for her."

"So communication is the secret," murmured Sonya half to herself. "The whole world changed because everybody began to learn how to communicate. The spirits communicated in dreams, and when they were listened to they returned."

"Yes indeed," replied Willowby, "that's quite correct."

"Absolutely everything in the world has a language, you just have to understand it," reflected Sonya. "How wonderful!"

The two friends lapsed into a comfortable, contemplative silence once more, allowing a deep connection to be forged between them.

Trying not to break the spell, Willowby whispered, "Silence is golden. Just listen to the silence. It is not what a person says that is important but what they do not say. Observe how they stand, observe what they do, this will reveal to you their true thoughts and their true feelings, more than any words ever could. The greatest communication takes place in the silence that exists between people."

Sonya enjoyed the silence; she looked around her, at the colours of each flower and the way that nature seemed to be alive yet absolutely still. "Silence is wonderful," she thought.

As if responding to her thoughts, the sun glistened through the leaves of the tree and cast its spell over the quiet little wood.

∞

Self-Talk

∾

The Girl who Lived her Dream

IT WAS SATURDAY and the sun was beckoning to Sonya to come and play. Remembering the conversation she had had with Willowby about the state of her room and the state of her mind, she looked about to check what state it was in. She decided to tidy up quickly as her mother would have wished her to do, before running out to play.

"I've tidied my room Willowby, and I'm free to play all day today," she called out excitedly as she raced up to the tree. To her surprise Willowby didn't respond. She peered at him curiously, a little perplexed. "Willowby, I've tidied my room just like you suggested, and I'm free to play."

Again there was no response. Sonya decided that Willowby must still be asleep and thought she had better leave him. She looked up at the sky, thinking how beautiful the sun looked that day, when a familiar voice said, "How beautiful the sun looks today."

"I thought you were fast asleep," exclaimed Sonya looking up at Willowby.

"Ah," replied Willowby, "I was engaged in some self-talk."

"Self-talk, what's self-talk?" Sonya asked.

Willowby smiled as he replied, "All human beings have conversations with themselves. I call this self-talk."

Sonya laughed, "I do that Willowby, all the time."

"That's right," replied Willowby.

"What is so special about self-talk, what does it really mean?"

"Self-talk helps you to control the thoughts in your mind. Think back. Remember the other day, how you behaved towards Miss Crabface and how I told you that your thoughts can create your own reality?"

Sonya nodded.

"And you remember how harmonious thoughts can create harmony between people."

Sonya nodded again.

"Well, self-talk is when you are practising to control your thoughts. You see," continued Willowby, "what a person says to him or herself will influence who they become. For example, if you are often feeling a little fearful, you could begin to tell yourself that you feel brave. If you keep repeating this to yourself every day, then eventually you will change, you will become brave. So your self-talk could change your life, could make your dreams come true."

"Is that really true?"

"Oh yes," said Willowby, "I know of a girl who managed to change her whole life by simply practising self-talk."

"Oh please tell me about her Willowby," begged Sonya making herself comfortable at the foot of the tree and looking up expectantly.

A hush descended all around, waiting for Willowby to begin his story....

The Girl who Lived her Dream

A LONG TIME AGO, there was a girl, with all the qualities you would wish to find in a human being. She was kind, she was wise and she was beautiful. You see, she possessed that magical combination of kindness and wisdom which creates true beauty. Beauty which shines from within and out through the eyes, and flows through the graceful movements of such a being: This girl possessed all that.

Now you would think that if you were kind, you would know it; that if you were wise, you would know it; that if you were beautiful, you would know it. But that's not necessarily so. You see, there is such a thing as jealousy, the jealousy of others who recognise those magical qualities and set out to destroy them. Such was the case with this young girl. Her father adored her, which made her mother jealous of her beauty; her older brother, who was foolish, was jealous of her wisdom, and her sister, who was mean, was jealous of her kindness.

Unfortunately for this young girl, her father was often away on business so she was surrounded by people who resented her. Her mother constantly criticised her looks and heaped praise on her sister, her brother constantly ridiculed anything she said, and her mother and sister would laugh at his cruel jibes. Her sister was always finding fault with her and making up stories about her and running to tell her mother, so again she would be scolded.

She was a lonely sad girl. She believed she was stupid because her family kept saying she was, that she was not attractive as she was always being criticised for her appearance, that she was an unpleasant person because she was always being told that she was difficult and a disappointment. Because she believed all these things, that no one would like her or would want to be friends with her; she truly wondered why she had been born and what life could possibly have in store for her. She neglected her looks, she neglected her mind, and she kept herself away from people and stayed in her own lonely space.

Because life for her was unhappy at home, she would often take herself off for walks in the wood. She had a favourite place where she would always go; it was her own special place: a green, grassy glade surrounded by trees with a pool of crystal clear water. She would sit on the soft turf, lean her back against a tree, close her eyes and feel the gentle warm sun on her face. Here she felt safely protected from the hostile world, and her spine would absorb the strength of whichever tree she was leaning against. There were times when she would bathe in the pool and then stretch herself out on the grass to dry. She always left the glade revitalised, feeling whole, able to cope with the dark life she had to return to.

It was her fifteenth birthday. The day dawned, and was particularly still as if waiting for something to happen. The whole world, it seemed, was holding its breath. The girl entered the glade as she had many times and lay down on the grass, knowing that the soft turf would comfort her as it always had. The trees spread out their branches, protecting the sacred space. The white clouds above parted, allowing the sun's rays to reach down and caress her tired face and weary body. She fell into a deep, enchanted sleep. And as she slept, she dreamed. And in her dream she had a vision.

A beautiful being of light descended a sunbeam and stood before her, dazzling her with its shining light. Its smile glowed with a luminosity of kindness and understanding, emanating love towards the girl. Such love that the girl had never felt before but had always longed for, and she cried with the pain of what she had missed and with the joy of what she was now receiving.

The being asked her why she cried. The girl replied that she was sad and lonely and saw no future for herself in the world.

The being responded, "How can someone as beautiful as you possibly have no future!"

The girl replied, "I'm not beautiful."

"But how can someone so wise not know that they are truly beautiful?"

The girl answered, "I cannot possibly be truly beautiful because I'm not even a very nice person."

The being, eyes aflame, retorted, "How can someone who is so kind believe they are so unlikeable?"

The girl persisted, "How can you say I am beautiful and wise and kind? You don't even know me!"

The being, luminous with love, gently stated, "It is so obvious. You are a shining being and you light up the world around you, and your light penetrates the deepest shadows where darkness lurks. Those dark places are not used to light and find it painful, and so try to extinguish it. Your mother, your brother and your sister are full of dark thoughts and feel the pain of your light keenly; hence their cruelty towards you, and their efforts to deny your light and extinguish it.

"But true light, such as yours, can never be extinguished. Nature will not allow it. All your life, the sun has nurtured your light when you played and walked and rested in its sunshine. When you bathed in the pool, the water cleansed your pain. The trees have given you the strength you've needed and the grass has absorbed your weariness. Now the time has come; you are fifteen, and you are needed to shine as the being you truly are.

"You must now learn to believe in your wisdom, to believe in your kindness, and to believe in your beauty, because this knowledge of yourself will make you powerful and there is important work for you to do in the world. You have now come of age and you must learn to take responsibility for your precious gifts."

Tentatively she approached the pool's edge, leaned over and peered at her reflection.

"Tell me what I should do," implored the girl, her eyes shining with excitement and wonder at what she was being told. "I would love to be kind and wise and beautiful, but I don't see how I can ever get to believe all those things."

"It is easy when you know how," replied the being. "I will teach you a simple ritual which you should practise for one full phase of the moon. If you do this, you will transform yourself completely, and enter fully into your own unique power. This is what you should do," the being explained carefully. "Every day, three times a day, for twenty eight days beginning at the new moon, you must affirm your qualities. Three times a day, you must look at your reflection and repeat three times these three phrases:

"I am wisdom.

"I am kindness.

"I am beauty.

"You must say this first thing every day to your reflection when you wake, once a day to your reflection in the crystal pool, and last thing every evening to your reflection before you sleep. If you do this exactly as I have instructed, then at the end of the lunar month you will truly believe in your wisdom, in your kindness and in your beauty. Then you will claim possession of those rightful qualities and your power will be obvious to the whole world. You will shine and you will be loved and you will be revered and you will be feted. You will use your qualities for the greater good and you will help to make the world a better place. But beware, the brighter you shine and the more beautiful you become, the harsher your jealous family will be towards you. Have no fear. In time, your light will melt their jealousy and they will be in love with you like the rest of the world. Remember now, you are wisdom, you are kindness, you are beauty."

As these last words were uttered, the light being diffused into the sunbeam and returned to the sun.

The girl sat up and looked around. She was alone and there was no sign of any light being. Today was the day of the new moon. Her eyes rested on the crystal pool; it beckoned to her. Tentatively she approached the pool's edge, leaned over and peered at her reflection. For the first time in her life she noticed her smile and thought it looked quite pretty. She caught sight of her forehead which struck her as open and generous, and she made friends with the expression in the eyes that looked back at her. She began her journey to transformation. She began her self-talk.

"I am wisdom.

"I am kindness.

"I am beauty."

She searched her reflection for any sign of response. It gazed steadily back at her. She repeated her truth. The water listened. She said it a third time, and the sunlight on the water sparkled the truth back to her. She breathed in. She felt new, she felt strong, she felt different. Returning home, she was curious to see if anyone would notice any difference in her.

It came as no surprise that her sister was particularly mocking of her that evening, and that her brother cracked yet more of his sneering remarks. Glowing inside, she knew the truth about herself. She knew her secret and she whispered it to her reflection three times that night before sleeping.

When she woke first thing the next morning, she greeted her reflection three times with her truth and when she took herself off to her secret glade, she sang her truth to her reflection in the crystal pool.

Everyday for twenty eight days, she performed her ritual three times a day. Very soon she began to laugh and sing as she went about her work. She walked tall and began to feel sorry for her spiteful sister and her foolish brother and her awkward mother.

On the twenty eighth day she went to the glade to bathe in the pool, to stretch out on the grass, and to sing her truth and glory in her new self. Imagine her surprise, on reaching the glade, to find a stranger sitting there: an old man, with a long beard and a staff. The girl noted his noble face and his clothes which were old and flowing but of fine quality. He sat poised as if waiting for something. Feeling she shouldn't disturb him, she decided to withdraw and return later. Just as she turned to go, he called out to her, "Don't go. Come here and let me have a look at you."

There was something in his tone that impelled her to obey, so she walked towards him and stood before him and lifted her head and looked steadily into his eyes. He studied her face and searched her eyes deeply. Eventually he slowly got to his feet and bowed low before her.

"I am truly humbled," he said to her. "Never have I encountered such wisdom, such kindness and such beauty united in one being. My trusty guides were right. You are indeed a queen among women. You will be my queen; you will be the queen of my people and the queen of my king. There is a wonderful country waiting for you, but it lacks the qualities of wisdom, kindness and beauty, so the country is sad and poor. Will you come with me and nurture and heal my country? I promise you, you will be adored and feted by all."

The girl went with the old man and there was great rejoicing wherever she went. The king got to hear of her words of wisdom and her acts of kindness, and went in search of her. When he came into her presence, he was immediately captivated by her brilliance, and begged her to be his queen and help him to rule over the land.

Joy returned to the country; she reigned with wisdom and kindness, and her beauty was celebrated throughout the known world. It became the golden age. She bore children, who passed on into the next generation and the next and the next the qualities of her ageless wisdom, kindness and beauty. The people multiplied and travelled and carried with them the legacy of her qualities. Eventually they encompassed the whole world, and peace and harmony returned and was established forever and ever and ever and ever and ever and ever and ever.

୶

There was silence; the only sound was the rhythmic patter of the water carrying the memory of the story on its journey downstream.

"So, her life changed just because she changed her thoughts."

"Yes," said Willowby.

"So she became beautiful because she began to think she was beautiful."

"Yes," said Willowby.

"And she became intelligent because she realised that she was wise, and happy because she realised she was kind."

"Yes," said Willowby again.

"Then thoughts must be very powerful," said Sonya seriously, "I never realised that before."

"Yes," said Willowby, "they are your most powerful tools, but you must be careful how you use them. Just remember, your thoughts create your reality."

85

Sonya began to think, and as she followed her thoughts she observed her mind creating more and more ideas.

She felt an energy of excitement within her and an overwhelming conviction that she had the power to make anything happen. Now, she knew that all she had to do was put her thoughts into practice one at a time and she could create anything. As this idea struck home, Sonya felt her head begin to spin. Her whole life passed through her mind, revealing infinite possibilities to her.

"Sonya, where are you?"

Sonya opened her eyes. Where was she?

"Sonya," it was her mother calling her for lunch.

Sonya looked around; she was now fully alert.

"Sonya, where are you?"

"It's lunch time, I must go," gasped Sonya, leaping up and dusting herself down. "Thank you Willowby, that was wonderful, I shall always remember what you have told me today."

"Good," replied Willowby.

"There are so many ideas in my head, it feels like it's going to burst," she exclaimed excitedly, her hands clutching the sides of her head to steady herself.

"Good," repeated Willowby. His branches began to sway rhythmically to and fro as a breeze gently rustled up, overhearing their conversation. "Follow them, but be careful, see where they lead. Then you can come back and tell me what you have made happen."

"I will, I will, I will," cried Sonya waving to him excitedly as she raced back to the house, eager to practise her new insight.

∾

What You Resist Will Persist

∾

The Lonely Dragon

SONYA WAS FEELING A LITTLE FED UP. She wasn't going to see her friends all summer. It was the beginning of the summer holiday and the only other person she could play with was her brother Jack. Younger than her, he always wanted attention. So annoying could he sometimes be, that she often found it hard to resist getting angry with him.

It was raining and Sonya was propped up against the window ledge reading her book. All was quiet except for the urgent tapping of the rain against the windowpane. She looked up from her book and peered at the sky, and in the distance she thought that she could just detect it beginning to clear. Her face immediately brightened at the idea of being able to spend the long summer days in the little wood with Willowby.

The sound of footsteps on the wooden floor interrupted her thoughts. Sonya quickly looked back down at her book as her brother burst into the room. He sauntered over towards the window, eyeing his sister seemingly absorbed in her book. "Oh," she thought, "he's such a pain," she really had to try hard not to lose her temper with him.

"Hi Sonya, do you want to play?" he hovered over her, bending near to see what she was reading.

Sonya looked up from her book, ignoring him as her eyes scanned the room, thinking, "Perhaps if I don't speak he'll go away or even vanish into thin air."

He peered down at her book and asked, trying to engage her in conversation, "What are you reading?" Refusing to reply, Sonya returned her attention to her book. By now, she could feel that he was getting irritated.

Playing the commanding officer, he started to march around the room, shouting out orders to imaginary soldiers. Continuing to ignore him Sonya carried on reading. Marching over to the television, Jack grabbed the remote control, flicked through the channels and turned up the volume. Sonya took no notice and continued with her book. The next moment, he lunged forward and snatched the book from her hands. Almost dancing a jig, hopping from one foot to the other in front of her he then ran in circles around the room, waving her book in the air, taunting her.

"Give me back my book." Sonya shouted, grabbing at him. As she did so, she caught the side of her book and it ripped in two.

Jack looked startled and darted behind the chair with the remains of the book, cowering as some of the pages fluttered to the wooden floor.

"Now look what you have done, you're such a nuisance," cried Sonya. Shaking with rage, she bent down to pick up the loose pages.

Just then the door opened to reveal their mother standing in the doorway. "What is going on in here, you two?" she demanded.

"It wasn't me," protested Jack, emerging from behind the chair.

Verging on tears Sonya, looked up at her mother, showed her the remains of her book, and growled through gritted teeth, "He tore my book." Then, still clasping the ripped pages, she screamed at her brother, "You're nothing but a nuisance and I hate you." Her quiet time and her private world were ruined.

The mother looked at Sonya and then at Jack, her eye finally resting on the torn pages in Sonya's outstretched hand.

"I didn't do anything, all I wanted was to play," he whined looking down at his shoes.

"You are a liar," retorted Sonya, a feeling of outrage mounting inside her.

"Now now Sonya, I am sure you're both to blame," her mother intervened.

That was the last straw. Sonya had had enough. She pushed passed her mother and ran out of the room, heading for the back door. Slamming it behind her, she heard her mother calling, "Sonya, come back this minute and tell me exactly what happened."

Safely outside, Sonya leaned against the door. Breathing in the sweet fresh air, she looked about. Her head cleared and for a minute she allowed the tears to pour from her eyes and run down her face. Then blinking them away she noticed that it had now stopped raining and that the sun was just beginning to shine, its beams of light glancing off the dangling raindrops so the leaves sparkled with diamonds. She looked over towards the wood, where she could just glimpse Willowby shaking the diamonds from his branches. Sniffing back her tears, she wiped her face with her hand and slowly wandered down to him, her mother's words still echoing in her head.

"What happened then?" Willowby asked her, as she entered the glade.

"Oh Willowby," Sonya exclaimed mournfully, "it was raining outside and I was trying to read my book. My brother wanted to play and he kept annoying me. I tried to ignore him but then he annoyed me even more. In the end I become so angry that I couldn't control myself and we ended up arguing and he tore my book."

Willowby smiled understandingly and began humming a strange sounding little riddle, "What you resist happens to persist."

Sonya looked up at him perplexed, "What you resist happens to persist?" She echoed, "What do you mean by that?"

"Well," replied Willowby, "there are times when, if we don't face the challenges we could, they continue to confront us." He looked down at Sonya who looked completely at a loss, trying to understand what he was saying.

He paused and began again gently. "Let me explain. If, for example, someone like your brother wants your attention and you ignore him, he will persist in trying to get your attention in any way he can. What you resist will persist." Willowby paused again; Sonya was deep in thought listening to his every word. "You see," he continued, "your brother was frustrated because he wanted to get your attention and you were ignoring him, so the result was conflict. You resisted him and he persisted."

Sonya began to giggle. The vision of her brother persisting in clowning about to get her attention returned to her, and, looking up at Willowby, she grinned sheepishly.

"That's better," remarked Willowby, "if you ignore him then you must expect him to go to any extreme to get your attention."

Willowby smiled to himself as the memories of all the children he had known came flooding back to him. "Do you know?" he continued. "There are situations in life which will continue to persist if you resist them, until you accept them. I know of a country where the people suffered greatly until they finally learned what to do to put an end to their suffering."

"Oh tell me Willowby," implored Sonya, snuggling up against his trunk, eagerly waiting for him to begin his tale.

"Now let me see if I can remember correctly. It all happened a very, very long time ago," began Willowby. He drew his branches in around him as he gathered all the ancient memories into his story.

The Lonely Dragon

ONCE UPON A TIME, a long time ago there was a country that was once green and fertile with pretty running brooks, woodlands that were alive with birds and animals, and fields which grew every kind of crop you could imagine. The people were kind, happy and well fed; they loved to dance and sing and would find any excuse to call a celebration. As I said, all that was a long, long, long time ago. There is nobody alive on this planet who remembers that time, but it has frequently been spoken of in the universe.

At the time of this story, however, that country was unrecognisable for it was now a barren desert. The earth yielded very little and the crops that did manage to survive the droughts were then devoured by a ferocious dragon who inhabited the mountain nearby. The people were thin and hungry. There was not enough food to go round, and they had resorted to fighting each other. It was an unhappy time; there was a feeling of hopelessness and desperation everywhere.

It was the seventh year that they had suffered the attacks of the dragon; such was their despair and frustration, they even fought with each other as to how to deal with the problem. The final straw came one night when, after discussions in the town square had led to brawling in the streets, the deafening sound of the mountain exploding sent everyone scurrying to their homes for safety. The dragon was at large again. As the people cowered in fear they asked each other, "What on earth can the dragon eat now? It's devoured all our crops this year. All we have left are the roofs over our heads." No sooner had these thoughts been uttered but the dragon bore down on the town and licked every one of their buildings with its flaming tongue.

Tinder dry through years of drought, and built of wood and straw, the buildings ignited ablaze immediately. Grabbing only what they could reach with their hands, the people fled to the nearest open space. Once a barren field, this area had recently been turned to ash by the dragon. There the people stood together silently and watched helplessly as their town burned to the ground.

Long after the last flames had died away, long after any smouldering timber had ceased to smoulder, long after the last wisps of smoke had dispersed, the people of the town, numb to the soul, remained standing together in silence, deep, deep in thought.

"Well there's no use fighting anymore, there's nothing left to fight over."

"That's true, everything's gone now."

"There's nothing left."

Then a young voice piped up, "I've got a mug. It's not the one I like, but it was hanging by the door so I grabbed it." He paused then continued, "It's an ugly old thing but at least it's a mug, it'll work. We could always share it if we need to."

He was joined by another young voice, "I've got a spoon, look! If anybody wanted to stir anything in your mug, they could borrow it."

It was the voices of children that gently brought the people back to their senses. Gradually everybody looked at what they were holding in their hands, and started to laugh and joke about the different ways that they could put their objects to use.

"I don't know why I grabbed this poker," said one, "I don't intend starting any fires, I never want to see another fire in my life."

Everyone agreed, then somebody volunteered, "You could use it as a weapon."

"What's the point?" the poker man replied, "There's nothing to fight over anymore."

There was a murmur of agreement as they all nodded and shook their heads, contemplating the future that lay before them. It was late and the people huddled together for comfort in the ashen field and the night wrapped its dark mantle close around them for protection.

"What are we going to do now?" a small voice pierced the night with the question that was uppermost in everyone's minds.

"I've no idea," it was the voice of one of the elders that replied, "but what I do know is that it is late, we have had a shocking day and a decent sleep will do us all good."

"Where shall we go?" another small voice whispered tremulously, "we've got no homes to go to."

"We'll just have to sleep here," the elder answered, "together. We're all we've got now. We'll sleep under the night sky; the stars will look after us. In the morning, after we have dreamed, we will wake up with some good ideas. But now, let us all sleep and dream."

Soon every single person was sound asleep and the stars drew near to whisper dreams into their sleeping minds. At the bidding of the sun's first rays, the townsfolk woke to the chattering of the birds and immediately began to talk to each other about the thoughts and ideas that were weaving through their minds.

"We must hold a meeting where everybody can contribute their ideas."

Amazingly they were all in agreement and in a very short time they had organised themselves into a circle, eager to begin. Amazing indeed, for you must remember that, until the events of the day before, these had been people who only communicated by bickering with one another.

"We need to take it in turns to speak," a child instructed.

"How?" called out an adult, confused.

"I know," cried another child, "Whoever speaks gets to hold my bowl and then when they've spoken they can pass the bowl on to the person next to them and so on, until everybody has had a chance to speak."

"You can only speak when you are holding the bowl, that way it's fair," added another child.

"That sounds like an excellent idea," one of the elderly men said.

"Come on, let's get started then," another urged, "before we get attacked again. You start," he said pointing to the child holding the bowl.

And so the people developed a method of friendly communication by means of the "speaking bowl". In turn they each put their ideas forward.

"I think we should put up a fight," stated one, "we're all good fighters."

"Yes. Let's launch an attack, it's been attacking us for years," another agreed.

"All the strongest men must unite together to fight the dragon," declared one of the strongest men.

"Yes all the strongest men against the dragon," they all agreed.

"What do we fight the dragon with?"

"Bows and arrows!" suggested one. "We could make them, there are some new saplings growing where the old trees were burnt down, we can use them to make new bows and arrows."

So everyone dispersed, eager to make the new weapons. For the first time in living memory people began to work together. They were working together, united against the dragon. The craftsmen shared their skills, so that by the end of the week the strongest fighting men were armed with the most powerful bows and the swiftest most accurate arrows that had ever been crafted.

The sun looked down in wonder, "What beauty people can create when they work in harmony with one another."

A slight cloud drifted over his face as he contemplated the reason behind their new found unity. "All united against an enemy," he observed. "Well, it's early days yet, we shall see." And he let fall his sunbeams and watched them play on a child's head, the child of the "speaking bowl."

The strong men set off. Together they walked through the day and through the night towards the dragon's mountain. The mountain had at first appeared to be close by, but as they journeyed it seemed to remain tantalisingly beyond their reach. At the end of the third day they found themselves in a valley lush and green, with a lake and enticing bubbling brooks, the most beautiful they had ever seen.

The men flung themselves down at the edge of the lake and began to scoop up handfuls of the water, pouring it over their heads and into their mouths to quench their thirst. Others stripped off their shirts and waded into the deliciously cool water and larked about in the playful shallow brooks. All were soon completely cleansed of their weariness.

Then something brought all the activity to a standstill.

A single figure was making his way towards them. Winged white birds graced his shoulders and his flowing white robes billowed gently about him as he approached. By the time he reached the shores of the lake not a ripple stirred, so captivated were the men by the vision before them. He stretched his arms out towards them as he greeted them.

"Welcome," he said, "I see you have enjoyed the refreshing hospitality of the lake. I expect you are hungry also. Help yourself to what there is on my trees. There is plenty for all, and I am sure all my friends will enjoy helping you."

No sooner had he finished speaking when one of the men let out a cry; a flying nut had caught him on the tip of his left ear. Nevertheless, he scooped it up from where it had fallen and began to crunch on it. Soon others were pelted with nuts; they ducked and tried to catch them as they hurled passed. At first they couldn't make out who their assailants were, until one man caught sight of a squirrel leaping from branch to branch with glee, his raucous laughter rattling out across the water.

"It's squirrels!" he yelled, "look at them all." The men started to laugh when they saw the mischievous squirrels taking aim from high up in the trees. They came out of the water and greeted their lively new friends, who swung and leaped acrobatically across the branches towards them in response.

"There are berries too, look amongst the bushes," their kind host informed them, "help yourselves." The squirrels chattered and beckoned the men to follow. They called to one another in delight as the sharp sweet juice of the berries burst in their mouths.

When all had had their fill, they stretched themselves out contentedly on the soft grass. Meanwhile their host was busying himself getting a fire going, and soon the sweet smelling smoke drifted over the men and they began to feel drowsy. "Draw near to the fire and keep warm," he urged, "look deep into the flames and breathe in their warmth. The wood burns for you."

So the men gathered near and gazed into the fire, breathed in its warmth and praised the wood.

"Tell me," went on the young man, "what are all these arrows about you? Why are you carrying them?"

"We're hunting the dragon," one of the men told him. "It's destroying everything. Unless we stop it, there will be no more food and we will die."

"We must kill it," another added, "before it kills us all."

"A battle then, I see," remarked the young host. "Do you know why the dragon is so aggressive towards you?"

"No."

"There's no reason," they all replied, shaking their heads, thinking back over the years of suffering.

"Oh there will be a reason," their host stated quietly, "there always is."

"I don't care what any reason is," declared one of the men, "the dragon is ruining our land. We'll have no peace until we are rid of it."

"How do you propose to rid yourselves of the dragon?" asked their gentle friend.

"Bows and arrows," one of the men called out. "Tempt it out of its cave, and when it flies and spreads its wings aim for its heart," he gestured with his arms. "There are enough of us, it won't stand a chance."

All the men cheered their agreement.

"Hum," mused the young man, hearing all this. Then he ventured, "Before you draw back your first bow, it might be worth asking the dragon why it is angry."

The fire suddenly spat ferociously. Few of the men heard his musings; they were tired, their heads were muddled, and they were drifting into sleep.

The next day they woke late. There was no sign of their host. Looking up, they noticed with a shock that the mountain was now looming over them, rumbling and smoking; it seemed to be beckoning. The band of men gathered their belongings, braced themselves and set off on their march towards what they knew would be that day's battle.

The sun beat down and scorched their faces and shoulders, and a chill mountain wind whipped them till they were raw. The clouds darkened and the mountain rumbled ominously as they approached. Suddenly their bones started rattling as the mountain began shaking and shuddering. Then an almighty roar and a blood curdling wail deafened their ears as the dragon hurled itself out of the side of the mountain into the air.

"Now, get ready," commanded the strongest man as the dragon began to circle above them. "All draw together, take aim."

The men took aim and the dragon circled down low over their heads, stretching its wings revealing the pale, vulnerable spot. "Let fly," came the order. A wave of arrows shot through the air towards a single, deadly destination. A light flick of the tip of one wing dispersed them, sending them crashing to the ground at the feet of the valiant men. The thunder clapped and the dragon vanished up a streak of lightening. The men, alone, stunned at their defeat, slowly retrieved their useless arrows in silence and retreated.

That evening they again found solace in the lush valley of the day before. They bathed, but this time there was none of the jollity of the previous night, they were all deep in thought. They gathered around the fire that their kind host had again prepared for them and drank the warm aromatic liquid he shared with them. Again they stared into the flames and drew comfort. No one spoke for a long while.

"The dragon's flames are angry flames. Why are they angry?" Was it the kind host's voice that floated up into the silence with the question that was haunting them? No matter, they all fell deeply asleep.

The next day the kind host and his animal friends furnished the men with nuts and berries and waved them on their way. They arrived home with their sweet offerings but little comfort to offer. The dragon was still at large; brooding and plotting destruction, they were sure.

That night the townsfolk all huddled together under the dark protective mantle of the night; even the stars concealed their glimmer. Dawn came and a horribly familiar cry shocked them all awake. The dragon descended on them, licking its lips, swooping low singeing all their eyebrows and eyelashes. The townsfolk cried in fear, they cried in despair, and when they had cried the last of their tears, they cried for a meeting. One by one they again voted to destroy the dragon, once and for all.

"We cannot survive if it continues this way."

They all agreed, but what to do? The precious speaking bowl passed around the circle.

"We need someone to creep up on the dragon and pierce its heart with a sword or a dagger," suggested a woman.

"That's right, but who?" And the women looked around the circle.

"It needs to be someone who is brave – a fighter who is not afraid to die if he fails," declared a woman looking directly at one of the warriors.

The warrior did not hesitate to step forward. A born fighter, he was keen to prove that he was prepared to die for any cause. "I will gladly serve this town," he proclaimed. "Just furnish me with weapons and send me on my way with a few trusted friends and I will rid this town of the dragon." He looked at the woman for her response and she bowed her head in acknowledgement. He glowed inside.

A week went by, and again the townsfolk worked together and produced the lightest, sharpest and strongest blades that had ever been made, and the warrior set off with eight trusty companions. They journeyed through the day and through the night until, on the eve of the third day, collapsing on their knees, they reached the sanctuary of the peaceful valley.

They marvelled again at the lush greenery and surrendered themselves to the depths of the cool, sparkling lake. The water welcomed them and refreshed their tired bodies and weary spirits. They basked, floating on their backs, gazing up at the beautiful evening sky. As the sun began to set, they became aware of soft, gentle movements on the lakeshore. There were rabbits bobbing about carrying bundles of carrots, lettuce and fruit and depositing them at the edge of the lake. Knowing it was for them, the men scrambled out of the water. Unlike the squirrels, the rabbits were timid and withdrew to watch their guests at a distance. In silence, everybody tucked into the food. The kind offerings of these shy little animals affected them deeply.

"Ah," it was the voice of the person they had been hoping would come, "I see my friends have been looking after you. I hope you have eaten sufficient."

"I've never tasted such sweet, juicy carrots," commented one.

"The lettuce is so crisp and aromatic," added another.

"How did they know I was longing for fresh fruit?" wondered a third.

"Ah," repeated their young host, "they are very sensitive. They sensed what you needed and brought it to you."

"Why would they do that?" the warrior asked.

The young host looked directly at him as he replied, "Man is a potential hunter and eater of rabbits. They sensed that you were hungry and so they brought you food. Better that, than you come after them to satisfy your hunger. That way your needs are met and they do not need to live in fear of you."

They all sat silently, deep in thought, struck by his words, and the young man busied himself with the fire. Soon the sweet smoke was encircling them all and they sat there breathing in the warmth and comfort of the flames. Eventually it was the warrior who spoke, "We're off to hunt the dragon tomorrow." The fire suddenly started to hiss and spit.

"I thought you had already tried that," their host remarked.

"We've thought of another plan, better than before," replied the warrior. "I'm going to creep up on the dragon while it is sleeping and pierce its heart with my sword."

"Let me see your sword?" requested the young man.

The warrior proudly drew out his sword, which gleamed in the moonlight; he stretched out his arm in front of him, admiring the sharp, glinting blade. The fire crackled and spat ferociously and everyone drew back a little for safety.

Then their host asked quietly, "Did you not learn why the dragon was so angry?"

"No, but we know how angry we are," replied the warrior. "Only last week it swooped down on us, terrifying everybody and singed our eyebrows and eyelashes. I mean, what will it do next?"

"Have you any idea why the dragon did that?"

"I expect it was angry because we went after it with our bows and arrows. But what does it expect? It keeps attacking us for no reason."

The darkness closed in and the fire burned low.

"There is a reason, there is always a reason, try and discover the reason." The company drifted into sleep as the words gently echoed inside their heads.

The next day they woke early and refreshed. As before, they found their host had gone, and the mountain, towering over them, was rumbling and smoking, daring them to approach. The warrior led the way. Again the sun beat down and scorched their heads and burned their shoulders, and again the chill wind whipped them till they were raw. The mountain belched smoke and shook angrily as the company made their way up the burnt, crumbling path that led to the dragon's lair. Their eyes burned and the stones slipped away beneath their feet. They staggered and dragged themselves up the steep disintegrating path, finally hauling themselves into the mouth of the cavern. Suddenly paralysed by fear, they stopped, unable to take another step forward.

Their warrior turned to them and said, "I must go on alone now. You must come no further. Thank you for your company, keep quiet and keep hidden." Then he turned his back on his friends and strode into the cavern alone. His companions did as they were ordered. No one dared to think, no one dared to hope. They cowered, hidden, barely breathing.

The warrior was grateful for the mask of protection that the darkness provided. The mountain shook stones down on him and a biting wind roared passed him, but still he moved forward. Again the mountain shook with rage and the stones fell and the biting wind roared furiously passed him, but he still moved forward. Again he was menaced, again and again, and still he went on.

Indeed, as the warrior put one foot determinedly in front of the other, he became aware that there was a rhythm to these occurrences. He breathed the rhythm, and in doing so he came to realise that he was experiencing the rhythm of breathing, the breathing of the sleeping dragon.

He reached for his sword and immediately the rhythm paused. A golden eye opened, piercing the darkness, eyeing its prey. The warrior froze. He was not yet near enough; he must not be seen, not yet. The eye closed and the warrior breathed again as darkness shrouded him once more. He took another step forward. A stone slipped, the eye glared, piercing the darkness again; once more the warrior froze. Once again the eye closed, darkness returned and the breathing resumed. The mountain shook, the stones fell and the wind roared passed, and the warrior moved forward.

Then silence. The warrior held his breath and drew out his sword; it gleamed in the darkness, lighting the path just in front of him. He took one more step and with a shock discovered he was standing right beside the enormous monster. In the dimness he could just make out the shape of the sleeping dragon. It was lying on its side, its left wing slightly raised revealing the soft vulnerable spot he sought. "A gift for the taking," the warrior thought and raised his sword to strike.

A howl of anger and despair almost ripped the warrior apart. The cavern lit up in flames and the warrior flung himself on the floor. A huge claw crushed him into the stones as the howling beast fled its lair. Silence descended. The warrior lay without moving for what seemed hours. Believing that his whole body had been crushed to pieces, he eventually summoned the courage to try and move his limbs. Although stiff and shocked to the core, he found, to his astonishment, that he was able to move. His relief at this discovery soon gave way to grief. He had failed. Struggling slowly to his feet, he hung back, loitering in the darkness not knowing what to do. Where was the dragon now? What damage was it causing? He was overcome with despair. Perhaps it was best that he remained in the cavern with his shame, and wait for the dragon to return and devour him.

His thoughts then turned to his fellow companions. Were they suffering? Were they alive? "If I have failed in my mission," he decided, "then I can at least help my fellow people." With that thought, he strode to the mouth of the cavern. He could find no trace of his companions, they did not respond to his desperate calls. There was no sign of the dragon. He looked about him; everything was eerily quiet.

Hardly able to breathe for grief, he decided the only honourable course was to return home. No sooner had he stepped onto the downward path, the mountain roared and rocks cascaded down around him and the wind ripped into him. He knew he had to flee and slithered down the side of the mountain, darting from the pelting rocks. Blind with exhaustion, he stumbled into the peaceful green valley. There he collapsed. He was not aware when gentle hands bathed him and dabbled his lips with liquid.

A fire spat and he awoke to see flames flickering and glaring at him. An overwhelming feeling of shame enveloped him and he drifted back into delirium, an agonising delirium of shame: shame that he had tried to kill a beast by sneaking up while it was sleeping; shame, that he'd failed in his mission and therefore would cause his people more devastation; and shame that his companions had perished on his account. His broken mind retreated into oblivion.

The sound of laughter and splashing water eventually persuaded his spirit to return. His eyes opened and gazed up at a bright blue summer sky. Heaven! He turned his face to the happy sounds that had awoken him. He couldn't believe what he saw. His dear companions and he were all in heaven together.

"So you finally decided to return to us?" It was the young host addressing him.

The warrior blinked at him, confused. "He was still on earth?" It made little sense. Then he smiled, realising he would see his wife again one day, and he began to dream of a wonderful new life where he would make amends for the past. Eventually he opened his eyes again and gestured for help to sit up; he was not yet ready to speak. His companions caught sight of him and came running over to greet him.

"We thought you'd never recover, but Solera said you would."

"Solera has been tending you day and night."

"He said you'd come back and he's right, he knows so many things."

Bursting with joy, his companions jostled with each other in their eagerness to welcome back their hero. The warrior looked up at the beaming faces shining down at him. "Does he know why that dragon is so determined to destroy us?" he whispered, shadows of agony engulfing him again.

"Yes, he does," replied one of his companions.

The warrior glanced up at his friend and remained silent, deep in thought. He was searching his mind for what Solera had said about the dragon. Gradually the phrases drifted back to him.

"Yes, discover the reason," repeated Solera, who had quietly approached, "that's what you need to do."

"How?"

"By asking."

"Asking? Asking who?"

Solera was silent.

"You mean ask the dragon?" The warrior was incredulous.

106

"Of course, that is the only way you'll find out."

The warrior was lost for words. Talk with a dragon? Had he not experienced such wretchedness as his failed mission, he would have dismissed the idea as utter madness.

"It takes courage, of course," stated the young host.

This was a truth the warrior recognised and could not deny. The truth pained him, because he realised that he did not possess the kind of courage that was necessary for this mission. As he admitted this to himself, his thoughts cleared and he remembered the heat of the dragon, its glowing eyes, its raised wing and the soft vulnerable patch exposed. A deep shock took root inside him, and shame returned. "How angry I must have made it, sneaking into its lair to kill it," he confessed.

"Imagine how you would have felt if someone had crept up on you in that way," Solera remarked.

The warrior leapt up. "It must have been furious," he declared, striding about as he gradually began to understand what had happened. "I would have been furious. It must be furious now. My goodness, what will it be doing in its fury? I must get back to my people, I dread to think what the dragon may be doing to them."

What sights met his eyes on his return home. Every field was black. As the warrior and his company walked towards the ruins of their town, a cry went out and people rushed to meet them.

"Thank goodness you're safe."

"We thought the dragon must have killed you."

"Look what it's done again."

As the warrior looked around, he noticed that the people who had gathered about him were all wearing headscarves.

"Look what it's done this time," his wife called out

107

from the crowd. The warrior looked as the young woman let slip her scarf to reveal a bald scorched head.

"It's burnt our hair away," sobbed an old lady, "what will it do next?"

They all began to cry, "It'll burn our bodies next, I'm sure. Oh what are we to do?"

They all looked to their warrior, who was too shocked to speak and unable to look his people in the eye.

He just managed a whisper to himself, "Their poor scarred heads, and all my fault."

Eventually, he felt a tugging at his sleeve, and looked down. It was the child, offering him the speaking bowl. Not knowing what to say, the warrior took the bowl. Everybody formed a circle around him and waited to hear him speak.

The words came to him, "It's my fault that you have been burned so appallingly." There was a movement of dissent, but no one could speak; they had to hear the warrior out, he held the speaking bowl. That was the rule. "Yes, it's my fault, because I made the dragon very angry." And he explained how he would have felt if someone had tried to kill him while he was sleeping. He then went on to tell them what he had learned from Solera.

"You see, we need to discover the reason why the dragon is angry. It's obviously been angry for a very long time. We need to find out what is troubling the dragon."

The warrior ceased speaking, relieved that he had shared his guilt, and placed the bowl down on the ground in front of him. He had said what he wanted to say. There was silence. The sun shone down and gently warmed them as they all sat there thinking.

Eventually, a child stood up and walked over to the bowl and picked it up. "We have to go and speak to the dragon," he said and passed the bowl on.

"I think we should all go together," declared the next child.

"I'd like to go because I want to visit that beautiful valley," added a third.

"Perhaps, if we go to the valley, Solera will tell us how to talk to the dragon," another suggested.

They all agreed to set off the next day, and busily went about preparing for their departure. The sun, having watched the bowl pass round the circle and seen that everyone had come to a wise decision, now felt able to depart and allow evening to settle in.

The following day dawned clear and bright. With the children leading, everybody set off on their mission. On the eve of the third day they arrived in great spirits at Solera's peaceful valley. The beauty of the place stopped them in their tracks. Never in their lives had they beheld such lush green grass. The children kicked off their shoes to feel the soft turf with their bare feet. They wondered how a place could ever be so beautiful. One child cried out when she caught sight of the lake with its sparkling brooks, and they all plunged into the cool water, splashing their faces and drinking deeply.

It was the children who first spotted the rabbits bobbing about bringing food. It was the children who started catching the flying nuts and scrambled out of the water to play with the animals and feast on the food that had been brought. They had never had such fun. The squirrels chattered with amusement as they watched the children clumsily scrabble up the trees after them.

Suddenly, playtime over, the animals dashed towards a tall, lean figure in flowing robes. The children followed curiously. This must be Solera. Solera looked at the happy faces clustering around him and smiled.

"Welcome," he said, "my little friends are enjoying your company, thank you for coming. It's been a long time since any children passed this way to play with them."

"They're such fun," one of the children piped up, "I've never played with wild rabbits before, we only ever hunt them and they always run away. It's much more fun playing with them."

"I never knew wild animals could be so friendly," a little girl added. "How come the animals are so friendly here?" she asked.

"They have never been hunted, so they have no fear, they greet all strangers as friends," replied Solera.

"If you don't hunt them, what do you eat then?" a child asked, voicing everybody's question.

"What have you eaten here today?" asked Solera.

"Nuts."

"Carrots."

"Berries and fruit."

People called out, licking their lips, remembering the delicious sensations of the foods they had eaten.

"Has your appetite been satisfied?"

"Yes," came the reply from all around him.

"Then you will feel no urge to hunt my little friends," continued Solera. "So they are safe and therefore they feel safe," he concluded.

"I like being friends with the squirrels," said a boy, "they're really funny and naughty and they're dead good at aiming nuts."

A little girl spoke out, "We want to make friends with the dragon."

"Yes," agreed another, "we want to make friends with

the dragon because we think it's angry."

"Yes," joined in a few others, "we want to try and stop it being angry anymore, but we don't know what to do."

Everybody fell silent and they all looked expectantly at Solera for an answer. He took time to respond, looking intently into the eyes of each waiting person. Eventually he replied softly, "It's very simple. Imagine that the dragon has feelings. Imagine that those feelings are no different from the feelings you have. If you were angry, like the dragon, what would you do? What would you want other people to do?"

"I'd want someone to talk to me, ask me what was wrong," a child answered.

"If I was angry with someone, I'd want them to say sorry," said another.

"There you are," he smiled at them, "you know all the answers."

"So we have to go up and talk to it and ask what's wrong?" one child asked.

"Yes," replied Solera.

The crowd, once more, lapsed into silence as they thought of this. Then after a short while someone asked, "What on earth should we say?"

"Whatever comes into your head," replied Solera. "If you have the right intention and you want to be friends, then the right words will simply come to you."

"I think we ought to bring the dragon a present to say sorry," a child suggested, "like a peace offering."

"Yes," everybody agreed.

"What could we bring a dragon?" and again they all looked to Solera for the answer.

He replied, "What did the animals bring you today?"

"Nuts."

"Fruit."

"Berries."

"And did that please you?"

"Yes," was the resounding reply.

"Would that be good enough for a dragon?" asked one of the men doubtfully.

"When someone brings a gift, does it matter what it is? Is it not the intention, the gesture itself that is beautiful?" answered Solera.

They all murmured in agreement. A ripple of excitement infected everybody, they had never thought in this way before! Suddenly they realised that they had found the solution to their terrible problem. They could hardly contain themselves. They were going to make friends with the dragon.

So sure were they that what they were going to do was right, that their fear at the prospect of meeting the dragon completely evaporated. They were filled with joy as their imaginations created visions of a wonderful future. They talked excitedly together that their land could one day be beautiful and fertile, and some began to remember songs about such lands in times that had long been forgotten deep inside them. That night they sang those songs and danced them, they sang and danced until sleep came upon them.

The sky was adorned in festive pinks, reds and gold, and the iridescent clouds parted to reveal the rising sun. The birds burst into a triumphant chorus and the people awoke to the spectacle of that morning's epic sunrise. Deeply aware that they were somehow responsible for the important role that they would be playing that day, they gazed, humbled, as nature revealed herself to them in her true glory.

The sun continued its magnificent ascent above the dragon's mountain and the people gathered together. They looked around and saw that the animals had assembled and a banquet of berries and nuts lay before them. Gathering up the food, they thanked the animals saying, "This is wonderful. We'll be able to take these to the dragon."

Solera approached. "There's enough for all; eat what you need, and what's left offer to Flamauria."

"Flamauria?"

"Yes Flamauria, that's her name."

"Her?" the people were astounded. "Her? It's a she?"

"A she dragon?"

Solera laughed, "Off you go," he said, "you don't want to keep her waiting."

"It's a she, it's a her," the people exclaimed to each other. Still finding it hard to take in, they turned and went on their way, waving goodbye and thanking their new friends. As they journeyed they could speak of little else but that the ferocious dragon was female.

"Well that explains a lot," declared one man to another.

"What do you mean?"

"The dragon, it's a woman, no wonder she's upset."

"What do you mean?" his friend repeated.

"Well," the first man explained with authority, "we've been ignoring her. You can't get away with ignoring a woman, they don't like it."

"That's true," another joined in. "Oh no, do you think she'll nag us?"

"That's what she's been doing all these years, don't you see? She's been so upset, she's been burning us with her tongue."

By now everybody was listening and nodding their heads in agreement.

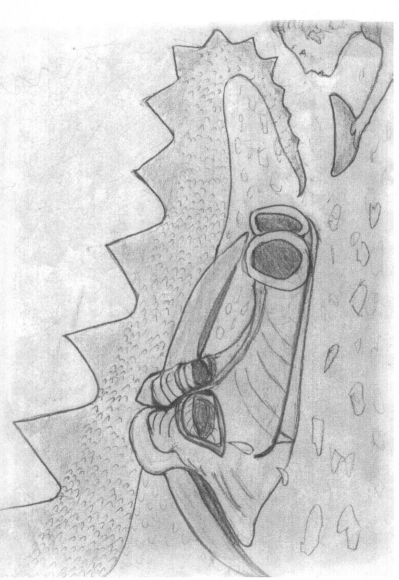

As he uttered the last few words, the little boy approached the dragon's eyes and placed the bowl in front of her.

"So what will we do then?" asked one of the youths.

"Do what you normally do," replied the man with the knowledge, "be kind to her, listen to her, love her."

"She'll be happy then?"

"Yes, she'll be happy then."

"Is that all? That's easy!" and the youth's eyes lit up as he thought of all the happy opportunities in store for him now that he was armed with this knowledge.

The men, confident that they knew how to deal with the female of any species, strode ahead eager to appease the she dragon in the ways they knew. This time the sun looked gently on and did not beat down harshly on them, and the wind did not whip them till they were raw but softly breezed about them, keeping them pleasantly cool. In no time at all, their joyous steps brought them to the mouth of the cavern. All was quiet, the mountain stood calm and still. The children wormed their way to the front, they wanted to be first. They were well practised in the art of approaching a mother whom they had upset.

It was the child with the speaking bowl who led the approach. Holding his breath, and the bowl out in front of him, he cautiously placed one foot in front of the other and entered the dark cavern. The rest of the company meekly fell in behind. Suddenly two blazing, golden lights illuminated the darkness. The boy stopped and allowed the lights to bore into him. Words entered his mind so he spoke them, "We've come to talk to you. We thought you might be upset about something, so we've come to talk to you."

All of a sudden, the lights extinguished and darkness descended once again. No one breathed. A moment passed. Then the lights appeared again, but this time, glaring with less ferocity.

"We're sorry if we've upset you, we only attacked you because we were so desperate," the boy continued as the words flowed into his mind. "For years you've burned our crops and we've had hardly enough food. Life has been very hard for us. Then you burnt our homes and all our possessions. We were angry and desperate. You were destroying us, so we thought we ought to destroy you." He paused, then uttered very quietly, "Sorry," and fell silent.

The lights went out once more and in the darkness there was a whisper of the saddest sigh as though the mountain was weeping. The people felt a strong breeze pulsing around them; their bodies began to heave with the rhythm of the breeze, and their tears flowed. The cavern lit up again, dimly this time, the two lights wavering before them.

"We are truly sorry if we've upset you," it was the boy speaking again. "We forgive you for burning everything down, we want to be friends now and live in peace with you," he paused. Then, "We've brought you some presents. Here," and he held out his precious speaking bowl, "this is our speaking bowl; I rescued it when our house burnt down and we use it whenever we need to discuss something. It's very special but I'd like you to have it now. I want to give it to you as a peace offering."

As he uttered the last few words, the little boy approached the dragon's eyes and placed the bowl in front of her. As he did so he looked up at the soft glowing lights and felt the tenderness of a mother's love flowing through him like warm wax.

"Is it my turn to speak now?" a gentle, melodious voice sounded.

The child nodded.

The dragon stroked the rough wooden bowl in front of her. "Thank you," she said, "it's a lovely bowl. I shall treasure it. Look," she continued, and drew out from beneath her a golden bowl encrusted with jewels. It gleamed and glittered in the dim light. "This is for you, a new speaking bowl, please accept this as my peace offering to you all."

The boy took it up. He had never seen such a beautiful object in his life, and he turned it round and round in his hands, admiring its exquisite craftsmanship. "Thank you," he said, "we shall all treasure this." Then he announced, "We've all brought you peace offerings, we thought you might be hungry," and he gestured to all his friends to come forward.

One by one, heads bowed, they came before the dragon and laid their offerings at her feet. Finally, one child, who was just about to place her offering, stopped and said to the dragon, "I'm sorry, but I don't know why. What did we do wrong? Why were you so cross with us?"

The dragon's eyes glowed tenderly and her warm voice resonated soothingly as she explained. "Long ago we were all friends, living and working happily together. Sadly, as time passed, people began to ignore me until eventually they forgot about me completely. In order to do my work I need your love and attention. You see, my job is to bring the light of the world into the heart of the earth and to guard that light and keep it glowing. I fly up to the sun and bring back light and place it in the earth's heart. I breathe on the heart, so that the light gradually disperses. Slowly it makes its way out through the surface of the earth and returns to the sun, encouraging all the plants to grow as it does so. Yet it is not just light from the sun that the earth needs.

"The earth also needs the light of her fruits, but, most important of all, she needs the light of her children's hearts." Flamauria paused as her mind turned to a time in the distant past.

"There was a time when people would bring these fruits to me with love and we would celebrate together. Therefore the earth's heart was rich with light, and she was able to bring forth abundant crops year after year. Sadly, over time people gradually forgot how the crops grew and began to ignore me and just took from the earth without ever giving anything back. Thus year by year the crops grew weaker and weaker and the land turned to desert.

"Eventually there was not enough food to go round, and people began to fight amongst themselves. Meanwhile the earth is dying. She needs the light desperately, so I had to go out and devour the crops myself. The crops I devoured were mean and bitter tasting because they were cultivated without love and because I had to take them by force. Eventually there was nothing left to take, so I burned your homes, hoping that you would take notice of me and respond." Flamauria's voice faltered as she continued with her painful story.

"It worked, you did take notice of me and you did respond; you came and attacked me. You did not hurt my body, but you wounded my heart. It grieved me deeply that we were now fighting each other, when we had once been loving towards one another.

"It was Solera who gave me hope. He knows the secret of how to live in harmony, and he told me that some of you had tasted the sweet fruits of co-creation. He also said that the water of the lake had cleansed you of your old ways, and that you would soon wake up and take notice of me. Good Solera, how right he was, here you are at last and you have brought me what I need, with love. Thank you."

Flamauria glowed with pleasure and her body lit up the cavern and her audience basked in the warmth of her presence. Eventually the child piped up again, "Do you mean to say, that if we come and visit you with fruit and things, then we'll one day have a land like Solera's?"

"Yes," replied Flamauria, "that is indeed what I say."

When the people heard this they started talking to each other excitedly, the children began to dance about with joy. Someone called out, "We must celebrate. Life will be different from now on. Come on everybody, let's celebrate. We can sing one of the songs we sang last night and dance to it. Remember?"

Everybody of course remembered and they danced and sang, and as they danced and sang the dragon's body glowed brighter and brighter, lighting up the whole mountain, and the festivities went on for hours.

Eventually, exhausted, everybody flopped down around the mother dragon and she breathed lovingly over them. As they lay peacefully asleep around her, she felt happy and complete. For the first time in centuries, she was full of love and felt a passionate concern for their well-being. They were her dear children and she would allow no harm ever to come to them again. She looked with remorse at their scarred heads, and breathed and breathed over them all through the night.

The following morning, when the people awoke and looked at each other, they marvelled at the transformation that had taken place. Their scars had completely disappeared, their hair had grown back and their eyes shone. The mother dragon glowed with pride as she gazed at the beauty of her earth's children. They turned to her, not wanting to leave, but eager to go home in order to transform their land and so return to her one day with their offerings.

"We shall miss you," they said to her.

"Look carefully at sunset and sunrise, and you'll be able to see me riding the clouds," she promised.

"When shall we celebrate with you again?"

"Celebrate whenever you feel like it," she replied. "Toast the sun and toast the earth, and dedicate fruit and flowers to me. Sing as you work, dance your feet on the earth's surface, and I will hear you and feel you."

"Do you have a birthday that we can celebrate?" asked a child.

"Oh yes, I have two birthdays a year," Flamauria replied.

"Two!" exclaimed the children excitedly, their minds immediately beginning to create pictures of presents and parties and food.

"Yes, one in the autumn and the other in spring. Everybody used to celebrate them, the days of balance, the time of equal day and equal night. On my special day in the autumn, people would shower me with gifts of fruit and thank the earth for the crops, and I would take these gifts and grateful memories to the heart of the earth. These happy memories would keep the earth's heart warm during the winter months. Then, on my special day in spring, when the earth begins to release the warmth of her heart's love-light, stirring all things to life, I would emerge from my winter retreat and there would be great celebrations."

Flamauria finished speaking and everyone was quite still, all lost in thought, each silently vowing to themselves that from now on they would celebrate

Flamauria's special days every year for the rest of their lives.

"Can we come and see you again?"

"By all means; come and see me whenever you feel it is right, you will always be most welcome. Remember me and acknowledge me, and together we will create a world of joy, beauty and abundance."

And so the people departed with joy in their hearts, singing and dancing. They celebrated when they arrived at Solera's haven. The birds and animals brought them seedlings to take home and, when the people took their leave, some of the animals and birds decided to go with them to help them create their new land.

Sure enough, just as Flamauria had promised, the land grew crops in plenty. The people rose at sunrise and greeted the dragon and paused at sunset to bid good-night, and celebrated their abundance and joy. They sang and danced on the earth for Flamauria and declared a holiday twice a year, and these two special days became known as the Dragon's Days. On these days when the day and night were of equal length, people would bring her gifts and dance her dragon dances, ushering her home to her slumbers in the autumn and celebrating her return in the spring.

Word spread far and wide about the transformation of this small country, and people came to marvel and learn the secret of their happiness and wealth. They learned the wisdom, and the universe rejoiced as those on the planet began again to acknowledge their dragons, and a new world was born. ❧

Sonya was looking up through the branches at the sun which was now shining brightly, wondering if she too could glimpse the dragon one day. "So the dragon had to nearly destroy the people completely before they took any notice of her," she reflected.

"Yes," said Willowby, "but in the end they faced their dragon, forgave each other and became great friends, so life prospered."

"Dragon Days," Sonya murmured deep in her reverie, "the time of balance, of equal night and equal day. Why that's, that's the ..." she struggled for the right expression as she shifted herself into sitting. She tried to continue as a memory deep within her pushed its way to the surface. "Isn't that the ..."

"The Equinox," confirmed Willowby.

"Equal day and equal night," Sonya continued, in full flow. "The day after the autumn equinox, the nights grow longer than the days, and after the spring equinox, the days grow longer than the nights."

"But on the two Dragon Days the whole world pauses. The day and the night are equal, light and dark are balanced, the in breath and the out breath are of equal length. On the Dragon Days," concluded Willowby, "the earth is poised for change."

"I see," Sonya responded, her memory now fully restored, "Dragon Days."

Willowby began to rumble a hum, and the breeze took up the tune and rattled his leaves to the rhythm. The brook babbled it out as it gaily bubbled across the smooth pebbles, and Sonya took up the chant.

"What you resist happens to persist,
Resisting causes persisting.
If you resist, it persists,
'Cause if you resist what's persisting,
It persists."

Eventually the chant subsided and Sonya continued, "So you can't ignore a dragon because it will always return to remind you, every year."

"Exactly," chimed in Willowby, his leaves bobbing around Sonya in delight.

Suddenly sitting bolt upright as a thought dropped into her mind, Sonya exclaimed, "Thank you Willowby, I'll always remember now. If the same things keep happening to me again and again, I'll definitely try and find out what's going on. I'll face my dragon."

Willowby looked down at her and smiled quietly to himself as he noted silently, "She's quick to learn, this one."

As if on cue, Sonya stretched and declared, "Perhaps I'd better go and see what Jack is up to."

"I think that's a very good idea," agreed Willowby.

She got up and grinned at Willowby, "I'm going to see how ferocious my brother's dragon is," she said, and laughed out loud as she thought of her young brother as a baby dragon. "Thank you so much Willowby, now I feel I'll be able to cope with Jack this holiday. All I have to do is remember my rhyme."

And as she skipped away, she repeated it over and over again until she had it off by heart.

"What you resist happens to persist,
Resisting causes persisting.
If you resist, it persists,
'Cause if you resist what's persisting,
It persists."

EIGHTH INSIGHT
Follow Your Dream
∾
The Dolphin Boy

SONYA GAZED UP at the sun; she detected a change in the atmosphere. It had been hot for days and days, and she sensed a weariness in the air. The birds were quiet, and the occasional hum of the bumblebees sounded dull. She looked up at the sun and thought that the sun looked different: it didn't seem to be shining with its usual brilliance. She then became aware of the weight of her limbs, an overwhelming desire to rest her heavy head, and a strenuous battle to keep her eyes from closing.

"Willowby," she eventually managed to whisper, "Willowby, how are you feeling today?"

There was a long silence. Willowby did not answer. Sonya felt that the whole world had dropped off to sleep. After a while she tried again, repeating the same question, between yawns, "Willowby, how are you feeling today?"

The sound of a slow, searing crack startled Sonya wide awake. It was Willowby stretching and yawning as he woke from a deep sleep. "Good afternoon Sonya," he yawned sleepily, "I was just having a little afternoon snooze. I was feeling rather tired. I always feel tired at

124

this time of year and often fall asleep at this particular time of day."

"Why?" asked Sonya, yawning.

"Well," explained Willowby, "it's getting towards the end of summer and it's natural to feel tired at the end of a season, and it's always good to have a little rest when you feel that tiredness coming on."

"Oh," said Sonya, "I've never thought of that before. It's funny you should tell me that this very moment, because I was looking at the sun while you were asleep just now and I was actually thinking that it looked rather tired."

"Yes," replied Willowby, "very good, that's very observant of you. You see, even the sun has a need to rest at certain times."

Willowby yawned and fell silent and Sonya felt a drowsiness creep up on her. In spite of this, she yearned for another Golden Insight. "Willowby," she whispered tentatively, "please can you tell me another story? I want to learn more."

"Ah, dear me now, let's see," Willowby yawned again, stretching out his branches once more, "another insight! Life is full of energy. Energy continually creates energy and attracts energy," he began, "and we colour that energy with our thoughts and feelings. Right now the sun is feeling tired, so I am feeling tired, and most probably the birds and the bees are feeling tired. Most of the flowers have already dropped their petals because they're too tired to hang on to them any longer. At this time the energy is about being tired. So as I said, the sun feels tired, so I feel tired, and I expect I'm making you feel tired."

Sonya yawned as she thought about this, and closed her eyes. It felt easier to listen and focus on what he was saying to her without the distraction of sight.

"When a person gives out to the universe, it always responds in some way. Just think about it."

There was a long pause, Willowby looked down at Sonya. Her eyes were still closed, allowing her mind to explore and challenge the explanations she was hearing.

He continued softly, and a gentle breeze took up his message, breathing it across Sonya's forehead. "There is boundless energy in the universe, full of opportunities and love. The universe loves because it loves itself. The universe loves, and works with love to help you blossom, and will give you anything to help that happen. Just think of the fruit the earth gives you. Remember the strawberries? And now the plums are just beginning to ripen, soon the apples will be ripe for you. The universe knows you need food to survive and provides you with abundance, enough to nourish you and enough to share. The universe will always give you what you want. Do you know what you want?"

Sonya had always wanted a swimming pool, and she suddenly burst out laughing as she imagined herself diving and splashing in the water with her friends.

"Take great care. You must know what you truly want because the loving universe will grant whatever it is that you want." After a moment's pause Willowby continued, "I know of a boy who discovered what he truly wanted and changed the world."

"Really," exclaimed Sonya, "is that possible?"

"Oh yes," said Willowby, "that is how change takes place in the world. That is how life evolves. You see, when people discover what it is they truly want, they focus their thoughts on that goal and those thoughts will attract ideas and people can act on those ideas. Those actions will create more thoughts which attract more ideas to act on and so on. Thoughts and ideas go on and on multiplying until the desired goal is established."

"So, you mean if a desire persists it will eventually happen?"

"Yes," said Willowby, "That is exactly what happened with the dolphin boy."

"The dolphin boy," repeated Sonya settling down at the foot of the tree. She knew this was a cue for the next story.

The Dolphin Boy

THERE WAS A BOY, beautiful and bright, but cut off from the everyday world. He couldn't participate like others, because he couldn't hear like other people.

He could hear no sounds, so he couldn't understand the words that were spoken to him, but he could often understand the meaning and the thoughts that were behind them, and these were sometimes different from the words that were mouthed at him.

Because he did not hear in the same way as other people, other people often didn't bother to try to communicate with him and this angered him and made him feel very sad inside. So sad, that he began to withdraw from the outside world and stay within his lonely self. He stopped trying to communicate completely, and he felt a darkness close in around him.

He stopped smiling, he forgot how to laugh, and the light in his eyes waned. His parents and family noticed the change in him and became worried. They tried everything to cheer him up and snap him out of himself. They began by telling him jokes and funny stories, that didn't work. They bought him exciting toys; even they failed to maintain his light. They tried the latest trendy clothes, but to no avail. The harder they tried, the harder they failed and the more desperate they became. They had grown to adore the light in their young lad, and their hearts were breaking apart as they witnessed the gloom engulfing him and extinguishing his exquisite light.

They cried and prayed for some help for their boy.

Then one day the newspaper was delivered as usual, and the mother collected it out of the letterbox as she always did. Wrapped up inside it were some freebies and fliers which she discarded in the bin, as she was wont, when a slim blue leaflet slipped out and landed at her feet. It was a luminous aquatic blue. She picked it up and reached automatically for the bin but the vibrancy of the colour halted her action. She glanced down at it, admiring the attractive colour of the glossy paper. The leaflet was publicising a new TV series and its accompanying book about the life of the oceans. She leafed through it, admiring the magnificent photographs of exotic sea creatures – they were really a feast for the eyes. She looked up. Her son was standing in front of her, looking intently at what she was reading and holding his hands out to take it from her.

She felt a stirring in her chest; this was the first sign of interest he had shown in anything for weeks. She held her breath as she placed the leaflet into his outstretched hands, and watched him as he gazed at his treasure with reverence. He took it away and sat down on the sofa, devouring the pages. As he turned one page, a gasp of recognition broke from him. He sat mesmerised, stroking an image with his fingers, fully absorbing the scene. His mother, looking on intrigued, tiptoed over to him and peered over his shoulder.

The photograph had captured a school of baby dolphins swimming and spiralling in a pool of light, the expressions on their faces radiating utter bliss. It was Jonathan's leaflet. He looked up at his mother, sensing her presence behind him. His eyes shone and he smiled with pleasure, and she returned his smile with heartfelt thanks as a sob stole up from her heart and lodged itself in her throat.

Jonathan carried this leaflet with him everywhere.

His shining self started to return; he noticed his new expensive toys for the first time and began to enjoy them. His mother sent away for the book of the ocean and this became Jonathan's most prized possession. He read all about the family of dolphins featured in the book. He poured over the photographs and gave names to each of the dolphins.

The series of the book came on the television. The mother taped every episode, but it was that of the dolphins that most intrigued her. Jonathan sat close to the screen, seemingly wanting to climb inside the set and join the swimming creatures. Every now and again he would reach out to touch the screen as one swam passed. They swam with great serenity, in harmony together, racing and leaping the surfing waves with such vitality and rapture that Jonathan would cry out and laugh and lean forward to join with them. As soon as the programme was over, Jonathan clamoured to watch it again immediately, and he watched it over and over again every day for weeks.

The change in him was dramatic. His confidence grew, his speech improved, and he developed a little

Once more he aligned his nose towards Jonathan's outstretched hand, and there the pair were, locked into each other's gaze, suspended in space and time.

patience for those people who tried to communicate with him. He pestered his mother to take him to meet a real dolphin in the ocean. His mother explained that that would be expensive, but said she would see what she could do. She asked around and searched the internet, and found a dolphin pleasure park a couple of hours drive away.

It was Jonathan's birthday and his parents decided to give him a special treat. They would take him to the pleasure park, and make special arrangements to have access to the side of the pool so that he could observe the dolphins more closely when they were not performing. When Jonathan found out what was in store for him he could hardly contain his excitement. He took his precious book with him. When they arrived at the park, he leapt out as soon as the car door was opened and ran to the gates to get a place in the queue. His mother had to stop him from pushing past everybody. He talked excitedly to the other children who were standing waiting, and generously showed them his precious book.

They took their places in the stands and waited for the show to begin. A shock of delight swept through the crowd; they oohed and aahed as the dolphins leaped and dived through their routine. As Jonathan watched, he felt a surge of joy flood through him every time the dolphins leaped through the air. He remained totally silent. After the display was over he sat quite still, deep in his own thoughts, oblivious to the fact that the crowds had dispersed and he and his parents were alone in the deserted stands.

Suddenly, "I want to meet the dolphins now," he declared, and they made their way to the discrete entrance to the poolside. One of the wardens ushered them through. A few other families were also there, but ignoring them Jonathan went straight to the side of the pool and crouched down. He called out to the dolphins.

The sight of him brought tears to his mother's eyes. What if the dolphins didn't respond to his call, how would he cope? He called again and she called out in her heart for them to respond to her son.

Again he called. The pool stirred, there was a gentle flip, and one dolphin appeared to present himself to Jonathan. Swimming to and fro, glancing sideways as he passed, he swam to Jonathan's outstretched hand and stopped, his nose aligning with Jonathan's face. He gazed directly up at Jonathan and allowed Jonathan to gaze directly down at him. After what seemed an age, he turned and flipped his tail and swam away. Jonathan remained still as a statue, waiting. Suddenly the water stirred to the sound of rippling and splashing as the dolphin, returning with his brother and sister, leaped and dived in unison towards him. Flipping their tails at Jonathan, they circled and rose before him, finally presenting themselves, noses aligning to the hand that was outstretched towards them. They gazed directly at him and he gazed back in return and the two species contemplated each other and communed in silence.

Time passed, they flipped their tales in salutation and turned and swam silently away. A long pause, suddenly the first dolphin was there again, gliding alongside. Once more he aligned his nose towards Jonathan's outstretched hand, and there the pair were, locked into each other's gaze, suspended in space and time.

Eventually, slowly, the dolphin withdrew and Jonathan was left alone, a statue, hand still outstretched, crouching at the side of the pool.

His mother approached him and gently took his hand. "We have to leave now," she whispered.

"He's my friend, mummy; he says come and play again. Can we come back next week? Please, I want to come every week, he wants to see me."

So it became a regular event. Every weekend Jonathan wanted to visit his dolphin friends. Usually his parents consented, but sometimes life demanded other things of them and Jonathan had to learn to accept that.

At every visit, the same dolphin greeted Jonathan, and his brother and sister would perform for him.

Jonathan's work at school improved. He took up swimming, at which he excelled, and he was chosen to swim in the school team. Jonathan's parents were delighted to see the transformation in him. His teachers were amazed, yet couldn't understand. But his mother knew the importance of Jonathan's connection with his dolphin friends.

His swimming continued to develop, he swam for the county now. Still he dreamed of going to meet and swim with wild dolphins. His mother encouraged him to fulfil his dreams, and she looked into the possibilities of taking Jonathan to swim with dolphins in the wild.

One day his time came; he boarded a plane and flew to a hot country. A boat took him to an island where he stayed, and a man with a fishing boat took him out to sea.

"Just call," he instructed.

The sea was a lagoon and Jonathan called, and called with his heart and sent out the love of the dolphins in the pleasure park. The water bubbled and rippled. They were there all around the boat, gliding, ducking and diving.

"Go on," said the man, "they won't hurt, they're inviting you to join them."

Jonathan took off his shirt and dived. He felt the shock of the vibrancy of sheer joy. It momentarily paralysed him, then he swam and plunged with all his might to keep up with his new friends. They swam alongside him, to encourage him, at the same time ready to catch him if he became too exhausted. He swam and played in bliss until time moved on, and it was time for the dolphins to move on with the tide. Jonathan hauled himself out of the water; the dolphins pointed their noses toward him in salutation, turned on their tails and flipped away. Jonathan waved farewell, thanked them and promised to return one day. The boat and the plane took him home.

Jonathan couldn't wait to visit his friends at the pleasure park. He crouched at the side of the pool to share with them his encounter with their wild cousins.

The dolphin took some time to come and present himself. Jonathan, at first oblivious to this change, told him all about his adventure. The dolphin listened and sank to the bottom of the pool, surfaced again and turned sadly away. Jonathan felt the pain, the longing, the loneliness, the suffering and the captivity. He crouched at the edge of the pool and wept. His tears dropped into the water. Immediately the brother and sister appeared, and the three gazed at him, saddened by his sorrow. They went through the motions of diving and swimming for him, but there was a painful vitality to their routine.

Jonathan spoke to their keepers about their sadness; he explained that they should be set free. They nodded in agreement but it was beyond their power. He wrote to the authorities, he wrote to the papers, he spoke on the news. Wild dolphins are wild, they need to be free. The papers printed his story and called him the dolphin boy. The power aligned behind his cause. People demanded change. They stopped attending the dolphin displays, the stands were empty, and the park lost money; so Jonathan had his way.

He boarded the plane; so did his three friends. He took them to the island. Heading straight for the shore, he called out to his wild mates. The surf bubbled, rippled and ripped apart with the excitement of anticipation. The wild dolphins were hurrying to greet their long lost cousins and welcome them back to the wild. He released his friends. Shy at first of the ocean, they needed a little encouragement. Jonathan waded into the surf with them. After a short while they responded to the calls of their cousins and swam out to join them.

The fisherman took Jonathan out in his boat and they followed the school. They were free. Jonathan dived from the boat and swam with them. They encircled him and played with him for an age and their rapture penetrated his soul. Then time moved on and they all swam off on the tide, all save three. Three remained and followed the boat back to shore. "Take us, we'll come back with you, we'll help others like you. Just for a year, then return us to the ocean," they sang.

So they came with Jonathan and he took them to the pleasure park. Word spread, the newspapers came, the television came and the crowds flocked to the stands; the park was thriving again. Three dolphins had come to stay for a year; they swam and leaped, infecting the crowds with the joy of the wild. The families came and the people healed, and the year passed.

Jonathan did as he had promised and returned the dolphins to the ocean. Their family was there to greet them all. Again he swam amongst them and again three more presented themselves to him saying, "It's our turn now, take us, we'll help, we'll come for this year, but only one year, then return us to the ocean."

Year after year it continued. Three dolphins would surrender themselves, to connect the people to nature, to the rhythms of the wild. The human race could borrow the dolphins, just for a while. The ocean would release the dolphins, for a certain time, in an attempt to bring all the worlds into harmony.

Jonathan continued his lifework. He was the guardian of the dolphins, he ran the pleasure park, he helped heal those who were stuck in their sadness.

He was the dolphin man, connecting society with the voice of the wild. At the pleasure park, people now learned that nature would always provide for their deepest needs, but that mankind must give back. Borrow, not steal or take away, for then nature could always provide with abundance.

❧

Sonya lay at the foot of the tree as the story came to an end. For the first time, she understood how nurturing nature could be. She remembered the strawberries earlier in the summer; she looked up through the branches of the tree and appreciated the cool shade it provided for her. She realised fully at that moment how wonderful nature was and how, like the dolphin boy, she needed to look after nature and give back to it whenever she could. She thought about how the dolphin boy's life had been transformed by that book about the ocean, and she thought about how he had succeeded in freeing the dolphins and changing people's understanding of the dolphins' plight. She lay there wondering what her mission in life would be, and wondering when and how she would discover that mission. Time caught up with her. She stretched, knowing it was time for tea, and realising that she would probably have to wait for another day to discover her mission. She sighed as she got up.

"Willowby, how fantastic that one person's dream can affect so many people and create such change."

"Yes, that is the power of following your dream."

"Whenever I think of that I will always remember the dolphin boy." She smiled to herself and then said quietly, "Thank you Willowby."

NINTH INSIGHT
Life is a Story
~

The White Winged Unicorn

THE DAY WAS SLIGHTLY OVERCAST as the sun was taking a rest. Willowby's leafy cloak billowed in the wind. Sonya strode out of the house towards the garden gate. Hurrying along the path through the trees she approached the willow tree. Glancing back over her shoulder, she looked to see if Jack was following her. She heaved a huge sigh of relief when she saw that he was nowhere in sight, and flopped onto the grassy verge beside the brook.

"Who's that?" asked Willowby surprised by the loud thump he'd felt at the base of his trunk.

"It's me Willowby," Sonya replied. "Who do you think?" she added, slightly put out that he would have to ask by now.

"Ah yes, so it is," he chuckled. "Jack not with you today?"

"No," replied Sonya, feeling curiously guilty.

Willowby coughed and then cleared his throat, and Sonya's cheeks burned as the memories of the argument flooded her mind. She felt her face turn to look up at her towering friend. The warmth in the kindly eyes that gazed down on her cheered her.

The prickly irritation she felt inside her began to

soften, and Willowby's deep whispering tones warmed her spirit as he gently began to speak. "You cannot control other people's behaviour; the only person you can control is yourself." He paused to allow this idea to sink in before continuing, "Remember, your life is a story made up of patterns; patterns of different thoughts, feelings and actions." As if to illustrate his point, he began to twirl his branches, making patterns, in the breeze. "You can create your own story," and the whole tree then swayed, gently swinging his branches together in a slow rhythm. "You see, you can create any story you want, and you can change it at any point," and as he swayed Willowby looked down at Sonya. She was listening intently, taking it all in as he continued, "Remember Sonya, your life is your own story. Other people have their own stories too, but their stories will be made up of other patterns. You can influence them but you cannot control them. You have to allow other people the freedom to create their own stories."

Willowby fell silent. After a while Sonya slowly nodded her head; she felt she was just beginning to understand and replied, "Do you mean like what happened just now with Jack?"

Willowby smiled to himself and looked quizzically at Sonya, "Tell me what happened then."

"Well," Sonya began, "I was sitting on the floor by the back door, doing up my shoelaces, when Jack appeared." Her mind drifted back in time to the scene.

"Where are you going?" Jack asked, hovering in the doorway.

"Out," replied Sonya determinedly as she continued tying her shoelaces.

"Can I come?" he pleaded in a whining voice.

Sonya pulled up her socks in irritation.

"Where are you off to?" he asked again.

That was enough. She got up and growled at him, "No, you're not coming!"

Jack retaliated singing, "I know where you're going, I know where you're going. You're going to that silly old tree, in the wood, the one by the brook."

Furious, Sonya glared at him, her face crimson.

"What do you do all day? I've been watching you," he taunted, stabbing the air at her.

Sonya held her hands back from hitting him and through gritted teeth snarled, "Mind your own business. Go and spy on someone else," and turning on her heels, she opened the back door and strode towards the garden gate.

Her mind gradually returned to the present moment as she tried to understand her story. "My brother was being such a nuisance," she looked down at her hands as she worked through her feelings. "He wanted to follow me but I wouldn't let him."

"Um," said Willowby, "go on."

"I was very angry, but ..." she suddenly stopped for a moment, took a deep breath and looked up at Willowby. "Oh Willowby, I felt annoyed and my stomach felt tight," she tried to explain clenching her fists, "and now suddenly I realise why I was annoyed." Releasing her hands from the tight grip, she looked up at the under-standing glow in Willowby's eyes.

"Oh?" he murmured gently.

"Well," she replied, "I always used to think that my mother preferred Jack to me because he's a boy, and that used to make me feel hurt and angry. But I've just realised that was just a story, a story I created out of my own feelings. I can see now that it doesn't have to be like that. I can change my story." Sonya looked up at Willowby, relieved, and then added with surprise, "I suddenly feel completely different, I don't feel annoyed anymore."

"Good" replied Willowby, pleased with what he was hearing. "If people learn to understand their own stories, then they can learn to know themselves. When people know themselves, then they can begin to change."

"I see," said Sonya, suddenly feeling full of energy. "I feel free now," she spread her arms out and laughed out loud as she leaped up and danced around his trunk. "Life is a story and I am free, life is a story and I am free." She hugged Willowby's trunk.

"Willowby," she asked struggling to get her breath back, "am I the only person who knows that life is a story?"

"No my dear," Willowby smiled down at her. "There was once a boy who knew his life was a beautiful story."

"Oh tell me Willowby," Sonya begged and settled down at the base of the trunk making herself comfortable, ready for Willowby, and the familiar deep rumblings began.

The White Winged Unicorn

THERE WAS A BOY WHO COULDN'T WALK, so he couldn't play football like the other boys nor skate on the ice in the winter. Although there were times when he longed to run about like all the other children, he discovered that he was able to get about in other ways. Unlike anybody else, he could journey in time and space to other worlds and other civilisations. On his return from these wonderful places, he would tell the children of his amazing adventures. His experiences fed his imagination. He was gifted with his hands and would carve the most exquisite models out of wood or wax. He would draw the most beautiful pictures of what he had seen, whom he had met and what had happened.

The other children loved to hear his stories and look at his pictures and play with his carvings. Everyday after school, they would stop off at his house and he would tell them stories and make gifts of the models he had carved. So his life was full. At night he would travel to far off places, and during the day he would carve or paint what he'd seen. Then he would meet up with the children and they would tell him of their antics, who had won what game and who had been in trouble, and he would tell them of his adventures. So their lives were rich, enriched by imagination and knowledge.

The adults were astonished at the boy's imagination and skill. They found his pictures and carvings most curious. However, to the children this was no imagination, this was reality. They craved to hear more; they craved because these children had a hunger for knowledge and they learned much from the boy's adventures. They learned how the greed of civilisations had destroyed planets, and they learned how warring planets had destroyed galaxies. They learned of powerful rulers who had enslaved their people for thousands and thousands of years. They learned of great teachers who had been persecuted and hounded off the planet because their teaching had begun to empower people and the people had begun to ask questions about their lives. They also learned the laws of co-creation: how to create planets of bliss, where knowledge was shared, where people looked after one another, and where the universe sang and every aspect of creation lived in harmony. The children longed to go there.

The boy's stories brought new knowledge to these children, knowledge that they didn't learn at school or from their parents; knowledge that made sense and inspired them and amazed their parents; knowledge that they longed to put into practice. The children would observe their elders. When these elders acted unwisely or made foolish decisions, they would reprimand them with a story from some lost planet or galaxy. Such an impact would these reprimands make that their parents would change their ways. Such was the power of the stories that the little boy brought back.

Of all the children who used to visit the boy, there was one child who, to him, was special. She was small and quiet and would just look at him and smile gratefully whenever he'd finished a tale. Very thin and a little sad looking, she was often the last to leave. She never talked about her parents and the boy had never met them. He noticed that when other children talked of their homes, she would fall silent and look down. She always wanted to hear about the planets of paradise, and she always asked the boy if he thought it would be possible to bring that sort of happiness to this world. He would always reply, "Yes, try it at home," and her eyes would drop to the ground. "Practise with the mice in the garden or the worms in the earth," and her face would brighten and she would nod and turn to leave, smiling gratefully.

One day she was sitting looking particularly sad, so he told her of his adventures and how he travelled to paradise. He told the girl of the white winged unicorn that had carried him there and he showed the girl the delicate wax model he had carved. The little girl reached out to touch it and the boy said, "It's for you, take it, it's a present."

She gasped and her eyes lit up. "It's beautiful," she said and took it gently and reverently. Turning it over in her hand, admiring the exquisite craftsmanship, she held it up in front of her and asked if a winged unicorn could take her to paradise.

The boy replied, "Yes, in your dreams anything can happen."

"Thank you," she said, "how did you know it was my birthday?"

"I didn't," replied the boy. "I just felt like giving you a present today."

"Well this is the only present I've had and it's beautiful. I love it and I will look after it for ever. Thank you, and thank you for the lovely story today." She blushed and turned to go, but turning back to him, she blurted out, "Will you be my best friend?"

The boy glowed. No one had ever asked him to be their best friend. He was too different. At that moment he realised how lonely he had been feeling all these years. He suddenly felt full of a new kind of happiness. This little girl wanted him to be her best friend. "Yes," he replied, "yes of course I will." And he smiled at her happily as he watched her skip down the road home.

Life was different now, bright and happy. In his dreams he often travelled to the planets of paradise and love, because he knew this is what his friend wanted to hear about. Everyday they would talk together about how they could make a paradise planet of their own, and the long summer days passed happily for them both. One day she was a little quiet and very thoughtful; she brought him a present, a white candle. The priest at school, who had just blessed her and who had given her her name, had given her the candle. He had told her that it represented her soul and that her soul was like the candle's flame. He told her that the candle was very special and that she should always keep it somewhere safe and light it from time to time, because then it would remind her of who she really was.

"I want to give it to you to keep," she said, "because you are my special friend." The little boy was very moved, he felt like crying. He had never been given a present out of love, and he suddenly realised how wonderful it felt to be special to someone. The little girl also told him that she was going away, because she had a nasty cough and she was being sent somewhere in the mountains to get better. She said to him that she was allowed to take a few of her possessions with her and that she was going to take the white winged unicorn he had given her, so she could think of him. And she wanted him to have her candle so he could think of her.

The boy was stunned to hear that she was ill, though he had always thought that she'd looked poorly. Now he realised how lonely he would feel not having her visit him. He also realised how much happier he had felt over the summer, knowing that he was her best friend. He promised her that he would light the candle for a few minutes before falling asleep at night and then in his dreams he would meet up with her. Her face lit up when she heard this, and she nodded and said that she would remember that. She said goodbye and turned and walked slowly away. The boy looked on after her until she was out of sight. She didn't turn back once, and he felt the loneliness that her parting brought them.

Sure enough that night, as he had promised, before falling asleep, he placed the candle in a special place beside his bed where he could reach it, and lit it. He gazed at its burning flame for several minutes and in the flame he saw the image of his little friend smiling at him. He smiled back, and said goodnight and blew the candle out. He fell deeply asleep into his dreams.

Leaving his tired body behind, he flew out of the window across the village to a tumbledown hovel. In the corner of a dark attic room, his little friend lay coughing and coughing. He sat at the end of her bed and called out her name. She immediately stopped coughing and sat up.

"Oh, you've come to see me," she said, pleased to see him, "thank you for keeping your promise. My chest is hurting so much and I'm scared of going away. It'll be lovely to be able to talk to you."

She didn't ask how he'd got there all alone, without his wheel chair. It seemed to her to be quite normal that he was sat chatting at the end of her bed.

"What time do you leave tomorrow?" he asked.

"Early. My father has hired a vehicle to take me to the station, and then he'll put me on a train on my own, then I'll be met at the other end apparently. I've never been on a train before."

"Think of it as an adventure," her friend said, "there will be all sorts of different people travelling and you can watch the scenery go by as you look out of the window.

146

It will look very different from around here, you'll see."
And they chatted until the boy felt that dawn was
preparing to break. "Goodbye," he said, "I'll come and
see you tomorrow and you can tell me all about your
journey."

She snuggled back down inside her bed and he felt
himself drawn back to the body lying in his bed at home.

The next day the little girl was taken to the station.
She hugged her father goodbye and found herself a seat
in the corner of a compartment by the window. Sure
enough, just as her friend had predicted, she amused
herself looking around at all the different types of people
on the train and she found herself making up stories
about them.

There was a fat smiling lady with a huge basket of
cakes and buns on her lap. Slumped beside her was her
grumpy son who glowered at the little girl every time she
looked over at him. She imagined the lady setting up a
stall in a market with all her bakery and accidentally
selling her son off as a lump of sourdough.

An unsmiling man with narrow eyes and a long
pointed nose seemed to be trying to listen in on people's
conversations. The little girl imagined that he was some
sort of government informer, so whenever he looked
over in her direction she studiously avoided catching his
eye.

Eventually, her curiosity satisfied by all her stories
about the occupants of the carriage, the little girl settled
down to entertain herself by looking out of the window
at the passing scenery. She found that everything her
friend had told her was true. She saw villages come and
go and caught snapshots of life as the train passed by. For
some time, trees surrounded them as the train plunged

its way through a forest. The trees eventually gave way to huge beautiful lakes and gradually the train passed into a range of mountains and began to worm its way round and up towards the sky. The little girl looked out of the window and gazed in wonder at the fields and lakes below. She had never seen such magnificent scenery. Enthralled by the beauty of it all, she imagined that she was truly on a magical tour, flying through the air on a sky train.

Eventually the train came to a halt and everybody grabbed their bags and bundled off. The little girl followed and stepped out onto a clean bright platform. She looked around as all the travellers were greeted by their families and departed. She waited to be found. A kind lady in a nurse's uniform came forward to meet her and picked up her bag and led her gently by the hand to a standing vehicle. The driver, who was a jolly man, leaped out and helped her in, and threw her small case onto the wagon and they rattled away.

The amiable chatter of the driver entertained the two passengers, and the little girl stared curiously out of the window at the streets they passed. It was obviously market day. There were people everywhere, with goods and animals, jostling each other as they went about their business. Leaving the market town behind, the little girl saw fields stretch out either side of the track for miles and miles until eventually the vehicle pulled up outside an imposing white building surrounded by high railings. The word "Sanatorium" was carved above the locked gates. Suddenly overwhelmed with anxiety, the little girl watched helplessly as the gates opened to admit the vehicle and then clanged shut behind them.

That same day the boy looked around at the children happily gathered in his garden. But without the presence of his quiet friend, the scene felt incomplete. He listened as the children talked to him about their games and the antics they had got up to that day. Today the boy did not talk. He kept quiet about his dream of the previous night. He waited for evening. That night he again lit his friend's candle; again her face smiled at him in the flame and again he bid her good night as he blew out the candle.

His dream took him to the solitary white building and to the room that his friend now shared with three other girls. She lay there tossing in her bed by the window, her white winged unicorn standing guard on the little table beside her bed. Again he sat at the end of her bed and called her name softly and again she ceased coughing and sat up and smiled.

"Well," he said, "this is a mighty fine place. How was your journey?"

"Just as you said," she replied enthusiastically and went on to describe the events of the day before. She told her friend of the beautiful gardens and how kind everyone was, but also how upset she was at how poorly some of the other children were, and how some wept because they missed their families and friends. He told her some of the tales he had heard about school that day, and so the night passed and again the boy felt the pull of dawn preparing to break. So taking his leave, he returned to the body in his bed.

Every night he lit the candle for a few minutes before sleeping and every night as promised he visited his friend in the sanatorium, and so the weeks passed and they talked of all the things that had happened and he told her all the stories she asked for. The candle burnt lower and lower, until one evening the boy noticed it was very low indeed. Nevertheless he lit the wick as usual and travelled to his friend in his dream. When he arrived at her bedside, he could see that she was suffering from a high fever, she was too weak even to toss and turn. Gently he called out her name and she slowly opened her eyes.

She looked up at him puzzled, "It seems so long since last night," she said, "I was scared you wouldn't come."

"I always keep my promises," her friend replied softly, "but we don't have much time left, your candle is nearly burnt out."

"No," she said, "I know, Annie left us today," and she pointed to the empty bed opposite hers. "She was so sweet and kind, but she was in such pain. I sat with her this morning and I told her your story of the planets of bliss. The story made her feel very happy and she said she would love to live there. I told her what you had told me, that she would go there one day on a flying unicorn, just like mine, and she closed her eyes and said thank you and drifted off to sleep. I sat with her and she looked very peaceful sleeping, so I didn't wake her when the gong sounded for lunch. I left her sleeping. When I came back later in the afternoon she didn't wake up. I know she's happy now and out of pain forever, free from that horrible cough and painful chest. I know she's playing on the planet of bliss."

The girl stopped talking and sat quietly thinking about what had happened that day.

She added, "I'll miss her, I'm upset, but I'm happy for her because I know she's free of pain and much happier now." She then looked across at her room-mate's empty bed. "You know I envy her. My cough is so bad now I can hardly walk. My whole body aches all the time and it hurts to breathe. The only time I feel well is when you visit me in my dreams."

"Come for a walk," he said.

"A walk, how? We're locked in at night. Besides, it's dark," the girl protested.

"None of that matters in your dreams. Locks never keep me out! Come on; let's go for a walk in the garden. Let's make it a sunny day with all the flowers out."

"How?"

"Imagine, then breathe in," and he took her by the hand. The little girl imagined and breathed in and gasped to find herself outside in the grounds. It was sunny and the birds were singing. She ran around breathing in the fresh air.

"It's so wonderful," she cried out, "I haven't been able to run for ages," and she skipped and ran around. "Race you to the lake," she called, and they raced and flopped down by its edge. "I beat you," she gasped trying to catch her breath.

"Only because I let you," he laughed.

Suddenly she sat bolt upright. "How come you can walk now?" she demanded, "How come you don't need your wheel chair?"

"How come you can run now?" he replied. "You can do anything in your dream life. I only need my wheel chair in that other life. That's alright. That's only one story; I can get on with other things in that story. But here I can fly," and he flew up to the top of the tree and waved down at her. "Come on I dare you," he called down.

151

Not to be beaten, the girl imagined and breathed in and found herself floating through the air to join him at the top of the tree. She looked around her, delighted. "You know," she said, "I've always wanted to ride on a cloud."

"Come on then," he replied, "there's one just passing overhead. Let's see if we can catch it."

And they flew up, laughing and tumbling over and over, clutching at the mist. Suddenly the little girl realised there was no need to hold on to anything, they could just float with the cloud, as the cloud. And as they floated and twirled the little girl asked, "Does this mean I can go anywhere I imagine?"

"Yes," replied her friend, "anywhere."

"I'd like to go home," she said, "I'd like to see my father. I think he's missing me."

"Come on then," he replied, "let's go."

The next second they were standing by the fireplace in the hovel that had once been the little girl's home. Her father was sitting in his chair in front of the fire, his head in his hands. Beside his feet on the floor lay the plate of a forgotten uneaten meal. Clutched in his right hand was a faded photograph of a lady nursing her baby. The little girl went up to her father and stroked his hair, "Don't cry Daddy. I'm having a wonderful time with my friend. He's taught me how to fly. I'll tell Mummy when I see her that you are missing her and she'll come and visit you."

He sat up and looked at her, "My little girl," he replied, "you look so well, so happy now, no nasty cough. This place is so empty without you."

"You'll have to find someone to look after you," she replied, "you can't spend the rest of your life moping. I'll see what I can do."

Then both the children felt the pull of the dawn.

They returned to the sanatorium, then the boy went on home to his own bed. The next day the boy felt tired and shivery, and he spent the day quietly with his thoughts.

That night he took out the remains of the candle, there was barely enough to light. Nevertheless he took a match to the wick and the flame burned brightly for a minute, revealing for a brief second the flicker of a smile before dying out. He stared at the burnt out candle and bid his friend goodbye, closed his eyes and drifted into sleep.

He felt cold in his dream and went in search of his friend. There were now two empty beds in what had been her room. Everything lay quiet and dark. His friend's bed was made up neatly, but it was empty, she was no longer there. He looked at her bedside table. The white winged unicorn was gone and he sat at the end of her bed and began to weep.

Immediately the room filled with a warm glowing light. He looked up and beheld, flying in through the window, the most magnificent white winged unicorn. On his back, glowing and laughing, rode his dear little friend. "Isn't he beautiful," she said stroking his neck. "He's just like the one you made me. I'm so happy, my mother is looking after me, but I wanted to come back and say hello. I knew you'd be here. I can come and visit you now," she said, "on my beautiful unicorn. Please don't cry, we can still be friends, but I'm happier now because I'm not in pain anymore. How's my candle?"

"All burnt out," he replied.

"Oh well," she said softly, "don't be sad. Remember me on this unicorn and you'll find me again," and with that she turned her steed and flew up towards the moon. The boy watched the white winged unicorn fly away high across the dark sky until it became a tiny glowing speck that passed behind the moon. The room fell dark once more. There was no reason for him to stay there any longer so he returned to his own bed.

When he woke the next day his head ached and his eyes felt heavy. His body shivered hot and cold; he sat up in bed and coughed, and coughed again. He looked at the remains of the candle, a white lump of wax, and he turned it over expertly in his hand and imagined.

He didn't go downstairs that day, he felt too unwell, but he heated his precious wax over the little stove in his room, and with some string he fashioned the wax into the most beautiful candle. The form it took was a flying unicorn. He worked for hours with great care and attention to detail. It was indeed a labour of love and by the end of the day he had created the most exquisite winged unicorn. Its elegant neck and soft downy wings had truly captured that which he had seen the night before.

Weary, he sat back and gazed at the creature he had created. As he passed his fingers over the intricate carvings he felt the tufty lump between the creature's ears.

It was a creation so beautiful that it was impossible to have the heart to set light to it. However, that night, the boy placed the unicorn beside his bed and stroked it fondly. He then took a match and lit the wick. The flame burned brightly. An image of a white unicorn looked out at him, and astride his back rode a girl he barely recognised, laughing and waving to him. He gasped and gazed at the flame for several minutes, before

154

. . . he looked up and beheld, flying in through the window,
the most magnificent white winged unicorn.
On his back, glowing and laughing, rode his dear little friend.

eventually carefully blowing it out and drifting into sleep.

He opened his eyes. The glowing white steed stood poised before him, "Up you get," he urged, "and I'll take you there." They flew through the night sky to the edge of the universe, into the next where the sky was pink. Floating in the pink sky was a golden shimmering bubble and they flew towards it. It was the planet of bliss, and the unicorn alighted on the grass beside a lake. There, bathing and sunning themselves, were the girl and an attractive lady. The youngster leaped up and ran over to greet her friend.

"I knew you'd come. Now it's my turn to show you around." She introduced the boy to her mother, who said how pleased she was to meet him and told him that she knew what a good friend he had been to her daughter.

They laughed and swam together and picnicked.

Then the boy felt the pull of dawn preparing to break over his world. His white steed flew down beside him.

"Hurry," he said, "we must not delay, there's not much time. Remember you can always come again, you know how, but now I must take you home." They flew through the sky into the universe of home and raced dawn back to the boy's house.

The next day the boy lay there coughing, and his mother scolded him for having worked too hard the day before. "Now look what you've done," she said, "you spend all day making this beautiful creature and now you're burning it. I think that's a great shame. You should value your skills more. Why you had to make that beautiful creature into a candle, I don't know."

He lay in bed all morning. His chest hurt and his head felt heavy. In the afternoon he sat up and looked out of his window and waved to his friends as they passed below. The children called out to him, but they didn't attempt to come up and chat. He was too ill, but he smiled gratefully and waved them goodbye.

That night he again lit his unicorn, and again in his dreams his winged steed appeared and carried him to the other world. Again he played and swam and walked and talked with his friend, until dawn pulled at the edges of the universe and he flew back home to his weak and painful body.

Everyday he grew weaker, every night he lit his unicorn candle and travelled across the universe on his steed. Eventually there was little left of the unicorn to light. He lay in a delirious state for most of the day; his mother sat with him, holding his hand and mopping his brow and trying not to cry. He gestured to her to light the remains of his unicorn. Tears running down her face, she did as he bid. He smiled and squeezed her hand and turned his face to the flame. He watched the flame flare fleetingly, revealing to him the flying steed, and he watched as the flame flickered and died away. He closed his eyes and sighed deeply and waited for his dream to come. Sure enough his winged steed did not fail him. This time he was accompanied by another, on whose back rode the boy's happy young friend. "I've come to fetch you," she whispered, "you can stay with us forever now."

"What about my mother?"

"We'll look after her, you'll see. Give her a kiss."

The boy did so and his mother smiled and sighed deeply as she dozed in the chair beside his bed. He squeezed her hand and whispered to her not to be lonely, not to be sad, but to remember all the stories he had told her, for they were true and one day she would see that they were. He kissed her again and she opened her eyes and gasped. He mounted his steed and waved to her. The two friends leapt up into the sky and winged their way home, home to the planet of bliss.

∾

There was silence as Sonya watched a white butterfly hover from flower to flower. It reminded her of the winged unicorn flying from planet to planet.

Eventually, she uttered the question that was burning inside her. "What about the mother? Wasn't she upset that her son had died?"

"Oh yes, but you see, he was so ill and it was very painful for her to see her own son suffer. So in a way she was relieved, for his sake, that he was out of pain," explained Willowby.

"Do you think she knew where he'd gone?"

"Oh yes, I think she'd have some idea," reasoned Willowby, "she felt him kiss her and had a glimpse of him flying away."

There was a short silence as Sonya thought of this.

Then Willowby continued, "Of course there is another twist to all of this. Remember the little girl's lonely father?"

Sonya nodded.

"Well, when he heard of what had happened to the boy, he thought how much his daughter had appreciated his friendship and how she had treasured his beautiful carved unicorn. He dreamed of giving it to the boy's grieving mother. Putting on his clean clothes, he gave her his carving saying how happy it had made his daughter and hoping that one day it would bring as much pleasure to her. She was very touched, and wondered at the exquisite carving. She recognised immediately the remarkable handiwork of her talented son.

"'My son made another just like this,' she told the girl's father, tearfully. 'But it was a candle and he insisted on lighting it every night. It broke my heart. It was the last image he carved and it was his most beautiful. Thank you for this, you are most kind. I will treasure it for the rest of my life.'

"The girl's father comforted her and took to calling on her most days. In time they became firm friends, finding joy in each other's company, and one day they decided to marry and grow old happily together."

∾

Sonya thought about this deeply and after a long silence she tentatively ventured, "So you could say that the children's death brought happiness to the parents, in the end."

"Yes indeed, in the end, you could say that," agreed Willowby. Then he added, "You know, life is mysterious in the way it works sometimes."

Deep rumblings emanated from the tree and Sonya became aware that Willowby was quietly chuckling to himself.

After a while Sonya, her mind still working to make sense of all that she had heard, continued, "So everybody ended up happily?"

"Yes," replied Willowby.

"I liked that story," she concluded at last, "I think I would have enjoyed the boy's stories too."

"Oh yes," agreed Willowby, "he told beautiful stories. You see, he dreamed his stories then he shared his dreams and then he lived what he had shared. His stories shaped his life. You see how valuable imagination can be. This boy had a wonderful imagination and he used that to create happiness about him."

"Who are you talking to?"

Sonya leapt up and swung round. For a moment she was speechless, then she quickly tried to regain her composure.

"What are you doing, spying on me?"

Jack squinted up at her, "Who were you talking to just then?"

"No one," said Sonya, trying not to glance up at Willowby.

Jack looked back at Sonya, rather perplexed. She hadn't shouted at him yet. What was she up to? What was going on? Someone else was there, he was sure. He looked around, they seemed to have vanished. He could have sworn he had heard her talking to someone, but who? "I don't believe you."

Sonya felt confounded, she didn't know what to say, she was afraid. Turning her back on him she walked away. She didn't want anyone to know of her secret tree. That was her story and she certainly didn't want Jack in on it.

Jack watched her curiously as she walked away. She wasn't her usual self. Then he heard a cough. He ran around the old willow tree. No one! Was he going barmy? Suddenly feeling uneasy he backed away, following Sonya towards the house.

Willowby chuckled to himself as he affectionately watched the two confused children making their way back home: Sonya trying to work out her story, with Jack stumbling along close on her heels.

TENTH INSIGHT
Go with the Flow
∾
The Pearlboy

THE AIR WAS QUITE STILL and the sun was radiating the last of its warmth. Sonya was wearing her fleece, as the weather had now changed. She was under the willow tree, leaning against the trunk and twiddling her hair. They had become firm friends. Their friendship had grown as spring had turned to summer and summer now to autumn. The flowers had hidden and the bees departed as the days had shortened and the nights lengthened.

Sonya's hair glimmered in the final hours of that day's sunlight. She was giggling as Willowby said to her. "Life will always change: it will bring you many gifts, some full of pleasure, others full of pain. Nothing ever stays the same; remember that, Sonya."

Sonya hung onto every word he uttered. She felt that this would possibly be the last time that they would be talking together. She wasn't sure why she felt this or even why she felt sad. It was strange, very strange, as though very soon something would be missing from her life.

"Willowby, why do things have to change?"

"That is life's wonderful mystery," he replied. "We

don't always understand the reasons why. Just remember this: life will always change and you have to follow where it leads you. Yes," he nodded, "follow your heart; follow where it leads you, for there you will find fulfilment, happiness and abundance."

"Abundance?" Sonya frowned puzzled.

"All that exists that is good for you," Willowby replied.

"But Willowby," Sonya persisted, "you still haven't answered my question, why do things have to change?"

Willowby chuckled in response, "That is the nature of life. Life is a creative force. You cannot have creation without transformation and change. Look at nature.

"Nature is ever changing and transforming, just as the sun changes places with the moon and the days turn into night and then back again into day. So the months change, the seasons change. Why, just look at my glorious leaves! Haven't you noticed how beautiful they are now?" He shook his golden branches and as he did so some of his shining leaves fell about her. He peered down at Sonya as she looked around at the rich carpet of leaves at her feet.

"Soon the branches of the trees will be bare, but then the buds will appear again and the leaves and blossom will return, only for the leaves to fall once more and so it goes on, you see? That's life. It is continually changing and growing. Nothing stays the same for ever, unhappiness gives way to happiness, ideas come and go. As time passes so plans change and people alter, situations can develop and often force us to move on. Time does not stand still."

Sonya thought of the different seasons and how they changed from one to the other. She turned her head and looked down at the brook flowing over the shiny pebbles. As she did so, Willowby caught her gaze and continued, "See how the brook flows, Sonya? Life is just like this happy little brook, its water constantly bubbling and swirling and flowing. The flow is a great force and it will shift you in the direction in which you need to go. Sometimes," he lowered his voice, "you may feel like swimming against the flow. Don't, you'll only run into trouble. Mark my words, Sonya, always go with the flow."

Willowby dipped his branches into the flowing water. Some of his leaves detached themselves and floated off downstream with the current, never to return, as if to demonstrate the point that Willowby was trying to make.

Sonya looked up, she could have sworn that he winked at her. Tingling all over, she grinned delightedly in response. But his face had already disappeared and she returned her attention to the brook once more: mesmerised by the clear water flowing, rippling and swirling. It seemed to have a life all of its own. Willowby's leaves, far away on their voyage, eventually floated out of sight. Breathing in these precious moments, Sonya absorbed the rhythm of the life of the brook.

Willowby looked down at his friend, impressed at her ability to wrestle with the ideas he presented to her. Once again he felt a little explanation would help her understand how to live with the flow of life.

"Shall I tell you another story?"

"Oh, yes Willowby, please do." Sonya clapped her hands in pure delight as she settled down, crossing her legs and hugging her knees.

163

The Pearlboy

HERE WAS A MOTHER and she was blessed with three sons. She and her husband were poor but happy. They had everything they wanted in life. They loved each other, they had a simple home, they had three healthy children and enough food to feed them all. The father was a fisherman, and his small business was just able to provide for all their needs.

Things hadn't always been so easy or so happy. The first seven years of their marriage had been childless; they had tried, but no child had come and they were very sad. One day when the fisherman was out at sea, he was feeling particularly unhappy and alone, wondering why the Gods would not give them children. He leaned over the side of his boat and caught sight of his reflection in the water. He sighed deeply and said, "I am a good man. If you give me children, I will be a good father and bring them up to be good people."

As if in response to his declaration, there was a stir in the water. His nets became suddenly heavy and he had to use all his strength and skill to haul them in. Imagine his surprise when he caught sight of his catch.

Entangled in his net was a beautiful mermaid! He had heard tales of them before, of course, but he had never in all his years at sea come across one. Her eyes were like the ocean, her skin the colour of sand and smooth as a pearl, her beauty took his breath away. Then with a shock, he realised she was in distress. Her tail was tangled up in the net and she looked frightened. He took pity on her, and cut her free from his nets and helped her slip back into the sea. She was grateful to him and to reward him for his kindness, she promised that his dearest wish would be answered. As a token of her promise she presented him with the most exquisite pearl. Then with a splash she disappeared into the deep.

With great excitement the fisherman took the precious pearl home and showed it to his wife, telling her what had happened. She cried with joy when she beheld its beauty and her tears fell, caressing the jewel as it glistened in her hand. She placed the pearl carefully under the mattress for safe keeping. Nine months to the day, her first son was born. At the end of two years she had a second son and after four years she was the proud mother of three healthy boys.

The father went out fishing every day to provide for his family. He never forgot the mermaid who had granted him his dearest wish, and, in thanks for the blessing of his three sons, he would always release a tenth of his catch back into the sea. The sea in return always made sure he caught more than he needed and so all the growing needs of his family were met in abundance. His business thrived and they were blessed with health and happiness.

The three sons were very different from each other in looks and personality. The eldest felt the responsibility of being the firstborn. He organised his brothers in everything. Since he was the eldest, he always felt he should be a champion. He would therefore rig any game they played so that he would win and only occasionally allow his siblings to beat him.

He was most comfortable playing with the middle brother, who was a fearful little boy always looking to his elder brother for protection. The elder brother would take advantage of this and bark orders at him and he

Entangled in his net was a beautiful mermaid!

would always run to obey, fearful of the elder's wrath. The elder enjoyed the feeling of being in control and the younger, living in fear and wanting to be taken care of, willingly gave his power away. And so they got along. There were times when this arrangement irked the younger one. Every now and then, he would crave his own power, but he would be too afraid to rebel.

However, one thing united these two boys more than anything else, and that was their resentment and jealousy of their youngest brother. The youngest son was born a bundle of joy. As he came out of the womb he crowed with delight when he beheld his mother, and she fell totally in love with him. He was the precious pearl of her life. Although all three of her sons were most dear to her, the youngest was indeed the jewel of the family. He was carefree and happy and spread joy wherever he went; he did as he pleased, and the world rejoiced in his existence.

Whenever his father took him out fishing in his boat, the nets would be heavy, as if all the fish in the sea wanted to keep company with the son in the boat. When he went outside to play, the sunbeams always shone down to play with him. Whenever he accompanied his mother to the market, people always clamoured to buy her produce and offered to pay the best prices. This pearl of a son, with his sunny disposition, without a care in the world, always attracted abundance and prosperity to his family.

The eldest son strove to gain respect wherever he went. He took to studying and learning from books. He became very knowledgeable; he learnt about other countries, mathematics and the universe. People came to study with him, to learn to read and figure out numbers. But however learned he became, whatever titles and qualifications he gained, he was never satisfied. His youngest brother, with no education whatsoever, refusing ever to study with him, somehow was wiser than he and wittier than he and more knowing. However much people sought to study with him, they always adored to be in the company of his brother, to laugh with him and bask in his humour and listen to his beautiful voice.

The middle brother was never as learned as his elder brother or as lucky as his younger brother. He disapproved of his younger brother's carefree behaviour, and was jealous that this brother never seemed to fear anything. He got himself a good secure job managing the accounts of a local trader. He didn't have the guts to set up his own business, he feared the risks involved. This made him feel bad about himself, so he turned his attention away from himself onto his younger brother and reprimanded him for his lack of responsibility.

His young brother would reply, "Why should I worry? I trust life; life will always take care of me. So long as I am honest, kind and happy, I have no reason in the world to fear."

Hence the youngest bother followed his heart, he travelled in the direction his feelings led him. He was gloriously handsome, and he possessed a beautiful singing voice. At night he would sing and tell stories. He was wise and gentle and generous. People would feed him and rejoice in his company. There were days when he would bask in the sunshine in the boat and the nets would fill, or he'd wander through the woods and stumble across the treasures of the woodland and return home laden with fruit and nuts. He never went without, and if necessary he would give away his last coin or his only piece of fruit. "There is plenty for all" was his motto. He enjoyed life to the full and life showered him with gifts; he trusted in the universe totally and it responded with abundance.

The eldest brother resented the ease with which his youngest brother made friends. The middle brother envied his ability to attract prosperity so easily. They became jealous of the adoration their brother received everywhere and came to detest the atmosphere of joy he created wherever he went. The last straw was that, when their young brother was around, their spouses would have eyes and laughter for no one other than him. It made them furious.

Seeing their wives so delighted by their brother's company so enraged their feelings of jealousy that they plotted against him. They hatched a plan to rid themselves of him forever. They approached their father and offered to do the day's fishing for him so that he could take a rest. The father was delighted and as the three brothers set sail together he waved them off with his blessing.

When they were out of sight of the shore the two elder brothers executed their plan. They fell on their younger brother, tied him up and wrapped him in the fishing net, weighed him down with stones and threw him overboard, surely to drown in the depths of the sea.

They then concocted a story of how they had trapped a sea monster, and how their brother had been pulled overboard in the struggle. They returned home and broke the story to their parents.

What grief struck that family! The father became old and frail overnight and the light in the mother's heart died. When the fisherman fished, his nets were now nearly empty. Their bright little home became grey with the gathering dust. As there was now little driftwood to be found, their hearth grew cold.

War broke out in the country and recession hit the community. The eldest son lost most of his pupils to the war, and the business which employed the middle son collapsed and he was left with no means. Both sons now returned with their wives to their father's home. They went fishing in vain and struggled to make ends meet as the ocean refused to fill their nets.

Meanwhile, we return to the plight of the youngest son whom we left sinking to the bottom of the sea. He struggled with the nets and the rope and allowed the motion of the sea to help him. The sea turned him over and over, and he became dizzy. He began to feel hands pulling and tugging at the net; opening his eyes, he saw that he was encircled by mermaids working to disentangle him. Eventually they freed him and gently guided him up to the surface. They swam with him and sang to him to keep him company and to keep his spirits from sinking. When night came a storm blew up and brought him a beautiful white seahorse. The mermaids urgently beckoned him to mount, he did as they bid. They waved farewell and the white horse took off across the waves, surfing the ocean for days and nights, until the clouds parted company giving way to a heavenly expanse of blue graced by a shining sun.

The white seahorse graciously deposited him on a golden shore. It was an island of paradise. The son thought that he had truly died and that heaven lay all about him. He felt the warmth of the sun on his skin, the softness of the supporting sand and the delicious cool of the sea water whispering around his feet. He stretched and breathed and realised he was alive. He sat up and looked about. There were palm trees nearby laden with fruit, waiting for him. Suddenly hungry, he gathered all he needed and feasted on the shore of his new found home.

He erected a shelter and built a boat and made nets. The trees provided him with fruit. When he went out in his boat, the fish offered themselves up to his nets. Life was good, nature was providing, he was happy and he sang to the birds. They flocked to him to listen and join in, then flew across the island to spread the news of the Pearlboy's arrival. The news reached the birds of the palace. The wise man there heard their chatter and asked the king for permission to travel.

Guided by the stories the birds sang out, he eventually found the Pearlboy on the shore, surrounded by birds and wild animals who had totally lost all fear of human the hunter. The youth greeted the old sage and offered him food and drink and the old man asked him to sing.

And as the Pearlboy sang, tears streamed down the old man's face, tears of sorrow, sorrow for the sadness that afflicted his country. He told the Pearlboy that the land was sad, so the people were sad, so the palace was sad, and that at the palace there lived a beautiful princess who was near to death for grief. He had prayed to the guardian spirits of the land to send them a saviour. They had replied that, when the time was right, someone would be brought from across the sea, and the winged messengers would spread the news of his arrival throughout the land.

The sage implored the Pearlboy to sing and spread his joy, travel the country and sing and heal the land. They would travel together, visit the sacred places. They would sing at the full moon and the new moon and the turning of the seasons, at dawn, at dusk, in the valleys, on the hills, to the trees, to the earth, to the rocks, to the wind and to the rivers and lakes. This they did and it took them seven years. In seven years they healed the land. People began to smile. Laughter and music could be heard in the towns. The country was alive with the choirs of birds and the sound of singing wafted out of the palace. The Pearlboy had arrived and was singing in the presence of the dormant princess. The beauty of his voice pierced the depths of her soul and she opened her eyes, turned to the singer and smiled. It was a smile of recognition and welcome.

The king was overjoyed that his daughter was restored to health and that the land and its people were vibrant with the joy of life. He declared a national holiday, to celebrate the birth of a new era and the engagement of the Pearlboy and his daughter, for she had fallen in love with him. In truth, she had waited for him all her life. They lived happily together and she bore him children. In time he became king and governed over a land of prosperity and abundance.

Meanwhile, back at the old fisherman's cottage, poverty gnawed at the souls of the inhabitants. Their nets were empty. They lived on seaweed. They had barely enough to survive, no more. Life was hard and there was no beautiful boy to sing or laugh away their troubles.

War had ravaged the country, the crops had failed, and the two brothers were forced to venture further and further out to sea in search of fish.

They hated their life of fishing. Every time they were out in the boat they remembered their dark deed. Every time they returned home they were confronted with their parents' grief. There was no escaping their dreadful secret. In the end they could hardly bear their burden of guilt any longer.

The brothers had been out for three days and three nights and had caught nothing. They were angry and in despair. The ocean stirred up a cauldron of discontent and the night darkened dangerously. Hiding for cover, the moon slipped behind a black eagle cloud. The boat was tossed from wave to wave and finally hurled with a force of rage against a rock. Then the wreckage was dragged out to sea with two desperate souls clinging for some remnant of life. The demons of the deep rose and dragged the wreck under the waves which spat them out in disgust and chucked them to a whirlwind to spin away. Again the demons rose and dragged them under, and again the waves spat them out to the whirlwind, and so they journeyed until the storm had vented its outrage and abandoned them on the shore of a distant land.

The morning rays of the sun discovered the debris washed up on the beach. The brightness of the light sought out the darkness in their souls. The pain was overwhelming and they dragged themselves out of the light to a nearby cave, cowering from the searching rays.

There they were discovered. Their alien fear was deemed suspicious, so they were put under guard and taken off to the palace. Thrown on their knees at the feet of the sovereign, they grovelled before him, not daring to lift their eyes, and begged for mercy.

The familiar sound of a melodious voice greeted them and broke open their hearts as the speaker inquired after the well-being of their good parents. The overwhelming realisation of all the grief and pain their jealous act had brought upon the lives of their dear family so consumed the two brothers, that they plunged to the depths of despair and their souls were tortured by their guilt. They were cared for and nursed with compassion, and gradually the darkness that had lodged in their souls relinquished its power and abandoned them. Their shattered hearts healed, and the glow of love for their brother took root and flourished, satiating them until they became whole and shining with light.

They went to their brother, deeply humbled, to beg his forgiveness. The beauty of his reply moved them to tears. "The waves told me how you have suffered. You have borne the burden of your shameful secret for fourteen years and you have tried to atone. It so happens that the fates intervened on my behalf and created good out of your cruel act. They have worked with me all these years to bring about abundance and happiness in my world, enough to share with all who come in contact with me. However, first it is important that you take me home to my parents. Time is marching and they do not have long before they move on and give way to the new, for they have fulfilled their contract in this world."

The three brothers set sail in a magnificent boat of mother of pearl. White seahorses accompanied them across the waves and mermaids frolicked in their wake until they arrived in triumph on the shores of their homeland. There they were greeted by a crowd, which had glimpsed the vision on the horizon at sunrise and had gathered in awe to welcome them.

Word spread afar that the Pearlboy had returned. The wars ceased as people began to forget why they had been fighting. Prosperity returned, the crops grew and the fish returned to the sea. Now nourished, the brothers' wives bore children. The old parents saw their family extend into the third generation, and the day came when it was time to take their boat out to sea. All their dreams had been fulfilled. They gave thanks and returned the precious pearl to the ocean, so that, one day, it may be passed on and bring happiness to someone else in need. As the old mother cast the pearl into the sea, its brightness caught the light of the sun; the water splashed up in response to its treasure's return, creating a rainbow bridge to the heavens. The old couple joined hands and together they stepped onto the bridge and the soft, colourful rays embraced them as they floated gently up to their home in the sky.

❧

Sonya was looking up through the branches at the sky, "What happened in the end? Didn't the far off land miss the Pearlboy?"

"Yes, in the end he returned to the other side of the world and continued as king. He ruled with kindness and understanding, and lived for hundreds of years and had many children. He created a world of paradise, and the land still remembers that time to this day."

"What about the two brothers, didn't they miss their brother?"

"Yes, but not as before, because their memory of him now was full of love. They had learned to trust in life and not to fear it or try to control it, so life remained peaceful and prosperous. They all lived in harmony with the sea, and the ocean provided for all their needs, and war never again came to harm that land."

Side by side, the two friends were lost deep in their own thoughts. The only sounds were the urgent lapping of the brook passing by on its journey and the songs of birds calling out to each other as they prepared their flight to the warmer climes.

At last, sighing deeply, Sonya murmured half to herself, "Oh Willowby, I see what you mean," and she looked up at Willowby, "I see now and I think I understand about life changing."

The earth felt suddenly cold and damp beneath her.

She got up, but hesitated and looked up anxiously at Willowby. He smiled down at her, understanding completely. "Yes, go inside now. Don't worry; I'll still be here for you for a little while yet. You'll know when the time has come to say goodbye."

Sonya shuddered, not just with cold, life without Willowby? She didn't even want to imagine it. She looked up at him; yes he looked tired. She tiptoed away and looked back at him before entering the house. Yes, he was still there, half asleep, half awake.

Winter and the Long Sleep
∽

IT WAS EARLY EVENING. The sky was already darkening and a few stars were beginning to appear. Sonya had returned from school. The evenings were now chilly and she was wrapped up in her school coat. In the dim light Willowby looked larger and more imposing than ever. Sonya wandered in and around his branches, waiting for him to wake up – he had promised, after all, and she was burning with a question that probed her every time she looked up at the stars. Eventually she heard a stirring and the sounds of the familiar low tones, now slow and drawn out.

"Sonya, my friend, your timing is exquisite. Yes indeed," he mused, before continuing slowly, "our perfectly timed meeting shows me how well you are now flowing with the rhythm of life."

Sonya glowed with pleasure, "A compliment from Willowby," she thought. "Now that really means something."

But her thoughts were cut short. Willowby was speaking again, this time with some urgency. "What is it that you are burning to ask me? Hurry, we do not have long together now."

Sonya wondered whether Willowby would stay

awake long enough to answer her. She knew that their time together was fast running out, as she blurted, "Oh Willowby, I have been meaning to ask you. How does the Universe work?"

Her question was followed by a long silence; was it too late? She waited anxiously for some response. Had Willowby already fallen into hibernation? Just then Sonya became aware of a bright star directly above Willowby; it seemed to be growing brighter and brighter, bathing him in a magical glow of starlight. How glorious he looked! A smooth silvery sound flowed out of him as he began to speak.

"The universe, Sonya, is all about you. It is everything that you can see and touch, and everything that is beyond what you can hear and what you can see. The universe contains many worlds: the worlds of the past, the future and the present, and of parallel lives. The universe revolves according to a divine arrangement of ordered principles, and it takes many lifetimes to truly understand them all and to learn how to work with them harmoniously."

"Principles? What do you mean by principles?" Sonya wanted to know, intrigued by what Willowby had begun to explain to her.

"Well, a principle is a kind of law or rule."

"Give me an example."

Willowby yawned long and hard before eventually continuing, "Now, there is:

The Principle of Love
The Principle of Forgiveness
The Principle of Patience
The Principle of Giving
The Principle of Time..."

Willowby's voice trailed off into silence. Then he jerked himself awake. "Where was I? Oh yes, most important –

The Principle of Sound, oh yes, most important, The Principle of......" and again Willowby yawned and dropped off in mid flow. He shook himself awake and a few leaves tumbled to the ground. "Of course, we will cover these at a later date, when you are ready."

Willowby drifted off into a silent reverie and Sonya pondered on the principles that he had named. She looked up at him. His magical glow had faded as the bright shining star above had retreated, and she shivered slightly, becoming aware of the damp rising up from the ground.

"Now," syllable by syllable, Willowby was slowly dragging the words from deep within himself in his effort to explain, one last time, before winter overtook him, "it is nearing winter, the time of my deep sleep. Winter is the time to prepare for what we need to do next, to be ready for when the times change, when the buds appear. Just look around you at nature."

Sonya looked around her at the trees, the brook and the little glade, now bathed in moonlight. She knew she was hearing Willowby's final words of the season. "Just look. The trees have shed most of their leaves, the flowers are sleeping and the dark nights are drawing in. It is a time to let go and reflect on all the things you have learned over the past twelve months, and it is a time to plan for the birth of the new life in the year ahead when we can grow and move forward once more." Willowby fell silent and Sonya understood exactly what he was saying.

"The time of the deep sleep," murmured Sonya, suddenly feeling heavy.

"Sweet dreams Willowby," she whispered, "till next year."

"Yes indeed," agreed Willowby. "All willow trees sleep in the winter, we hibernate, just like hedgehogs. Everything slows down so we dream our dreams."

"I have never thought of winter in that way," Sonya remarked. "I always used to see the winter time as boring because I couldn't go outside to play when it was dark."

"Yes, you see," Willowby replied, "it is such a valuable time and most people ignore the beautiful opportunity that winter offers us." He paused, then stated, "Take your cue from nature. Nature is the perfect teacher, because everything in nature is connected, you only need to look."

Silence fell, as though all that remained awake in the garden was listening to Willowby, as his voice, now reduced to a whisper, urged, "Remember, look and everyday you will find a miracle, a sign that you are loved. You are surrounded by blessings. The sun will always find a way to shine, even when the clouds are low, and the earth, if you look after it, will nourish you."

Sonya looked around but only felt how dull life would be without Willowby to talk to. "So, that means I won't be able to talk with you through the winter time," Sonya sighed sadly. "I will miss you," she whispered.

There was silence again. They both knew that this time spell could not be broken. It brought a sweet sadness that the two friends felt keenly. They both knew that, no matter what might happen, whatever the season, the friendship that existed between them would withstand all the tests of time. For theirs was a friendship based on a wisdom that had blossomed during a summer of shared joy and laughter; between them existed a feeling of trust and delight in one another's company. Willowby was a wonderful teacher and Sonya a brilliant student. Together they had learned, together they had grown.

Willowby's voice was barely audible now, "I will always be here for you, just like I was for your great, great grandfather. I will be here for you and your children and your children's children."

Deeply moved by his declaration, she replied, "Thank you Willowby." He would always be there, and they would talk again in six months time. That wasn't such a long time was it? "This is goodbye then?" a tear slipped down her cheek.

Willowby gently replied, "Yes, it's time for the long, deep sleep."

She hugged his trunk and felt the slow pulse of his being encircled in her arms. His branches drew in around her and he blessed her, anointing her with his leaves. She gathered them up to treasure as mementoes of the happy hours they had spent together. Over the coming months they would help to remind her that spring would bring new leaves and new adventures, new stories and new insights.

"Sweet dreams Willowby," she whispered, "till next year."

The star high in the dark sky winked in reply, and a chill breeze crept up on her as she tiptoed away.

"Yes," it breathed into her, "till next year."